B
L
U
E

Volume 2

Dedication Page

This book is dedicated to my daddy (Ronald G. Smith- a quiet strength) family and friends who believed in me and pushed this second book becoming a reality. You guys encourage me to hold on and keep the faith!

To my late grandmother, Irene W. Stanback who always told me prayer is the key and faith unlocks the door.

To my now late and always beloved mother, Helen M. Stanback who is watching over us in spirit. She has always been our number one cheerleader and support. This one is for you!! I miss you like crazy and love you past eternity.

To my girls Tecia, Shawnell, Kalaeya (Aja and Kasyn included) remember with God all things are possible.

To my husband Shawn, I thank God for blessing me with you. Thank you for being my inspiration.

TO MY FANS!! I ABSOLUTELY ADORE YOU!! YOU GUYS ROCK!! STICK AROUND, THE BEST IS YET TO COME!!

I love you all!

Table of Contents

Introduction

Blue decided to give her best friend a try at love. She discovered that she was pregnant with Big's child when she realized how strong her feelings were for Mike. Wanting nothing more to do with Big, Blue and Mike made plans to spend their lives together not only as lovers, but as man and wife. Desperate that the attention is not on him anymore, Big demands rights to a child and a woman he didn't want or care about. They have endured harassing phone calls, a hospital stay, and several stalker moments. It is evident that Big was fixated on making their lives hell. Especially Blue's. She was his target in this long charade of cat and mouse. He stopped toying with her long enough to shift his focus to Mike. Even after the fights gone viral and the alerts of police Big was still determined to destroy not only their love but them as well. Mike vowed to protect Blue but Big was not making it easy! Between chauffeuring her back and forth, their high demanding jobs his with late night hours, baby showers and a wedding, Mike was beginning to run on fumes. He must relinquish her some freedom, but that task was hard when Big showed up in unsuspecting places. It seemed as if he couldn't be stopped and that they would never get rid of the monster that was created out of a love birthed by his ex and her best friend. It was clear he had to be stopped but how? In the game of life, someone has to lose in order for one to win. The sport was played, and it costed gravely. Can a fumble be recovered, and life continue with those who are left remaining?

Chapter 1

The workday was over, Mike met Blue at her house. He wanted to be there just in case Big came over showing out and stressing her. Mike is not a fighter, but he had been looking for a reason to lay hands on Big. He hated how he'd treated his friend and woman he was madly in love with.

"Hey guy. Thank you for the roses. They were beautiful. I loved them and I am glad you have not changed your mind about us," she spoke.

"I gave beautiful roses to a beautiful woman. Lady I love you. It is just that plain and simple."

"Mike, I promise you always know what to say. I don't deserve you. Especially under the circumstances."

"You don't!" he picked with her. "But hey you got me and here we are."

Mike took Blue by the hand and led her to the couch. He kneeled in front of her. He wanted to make sure he had her undivided attention. He made her look him in his eye while he held her hand and began to show her reasons why he the man she should be with.

"Blue, why do you think because are pregnant that my feelings for you have changed? Well they have not. I still feel the same for you as I did. Now I will love this child as I love you. Nothing has changed except what we shared that night. That only enhanced what I was already feeling for you. I will love this baby because it is a part of you. As a matter of fact, I have more than enough room in my house. Why don't you put your place up for sale and move in with me? What do you say? Not as boyfriend and girlfriend but as best friends not even with benefits."

"I say no. I don't know. You would do that for me Mike?"

"Do what? Offer you a place to live and help ease some of your stresses? I don't want to be with anybody, but you and the fact of the matter is I know how we feel about each other. If you would let me, I would be honored to write my name on the birth certificate and give you both my last name."

"Mike what are you saying?"

"Blue what I am saying is I love you. I want to be with you. When the time is right, I want to make you my wife and start this family. You and me and the baby growing inside you. He will be our baby. If dude don't want to be a part of the baby's life, so be it. We'll have him sign over all his parental rights and he becomes a distant memory to us all. We start putting motions into play so the same day the baby is born, I can sign the birth certificate and if needed adoption papers. I don't expect you to give me an answer right now. Just know you have an offer that stands. When you are ready, we can make it official, and baby or not, there is no other woman I can see spending my life with but you. You are my best friend and I want to share my all with you. We can put your place up for sale. Besides, I am not too thrilled about ole boy being able to just drop in on you whenever the mood hits him. I live in a five-bedroom house that longs for a woman's touch, and if you don't like it here, we can put both places up for sale and find something else. I don't care what we do Blue. My only desire is to be with you. I love you."

"I love you too Mike Long. I can't see myself without you either. The fact that you love me especially with another man's child is more than I deserve. Thank you for loving me so. I wish it had not taken all of this to come to my senses. The timing never seemed right."

"Don't you get it? The timing is right for us now. I don't just love you Blue. I am in love with you. Madly to be exact."

Tears streamed down her face. She realized that he was truly the man for her. Mike was who she'd prayed for. It took her a minute to grasp that concept. She could finally take herself off the market and stop the cycle of entertaining other men. The man who loved her knelt in front of her to profess his undying adoration and intentions. Every ounce of her wanted to reciprocate the love he had shown her for the past eight years.

"Mike I am in love with you too. These past few months helped me realize how much I want to be with you. I do want a fresh start. I am ready to move past all the hurt and pain that has happened to me in this place. I'd love to move into a new place and create new memories with you and this baby. I promise to make you happy Mike and share my world with you. I do want us to try living as housemates like you said just for the first few months. I want us to see if this is what we really want."

"Blue, just so you know for the past eight years you were the only one I ever wanted. I have been ready. I have been waiting on you. In a few months if this is officially what you want, we can put this diamond on your finger. We can have a small ceremony. It will be something quaint for just the families and close friends 'because I know you don't want to bring the baby in the world out of wedlock. And by the way I already know what I want, and I am looking at her!"

Blue opened the box and saw a five-carat princess cut solitaire platinum band engagement ring. She grabbed him by the face. She leaned into him wrapped her arms around him and kissed him passionately. They are excited about the transition that will take place in their lives. Blue got up. She relieved Mike from his knees. He stood up and leaned in and kissed her belly. He rubbed it and promised to love and protect the baby as his own. She took his hand and led him to the bedroom. He followed her lead. He wanted her bad. He was not sure he should just keep having intercourse with her while she carried the baby. He did it the first time and felt some type of way. However, if need be, he could surely rise to the occasion and handle his business. He had had his share of women. None had ever been pregnant so that took him way out of his element. But this too was different because he'd made plans for her to be his future wife.

"I just want you to lay here with me Mike tonight," she pleaded.

"Ok yeah I can do that," he signed in relief.

He took her in his arms, and they laid down on the bed. They talked about what life would be like together and what they expect from each other in this newly embraced capacity that made them an official couple. He wanted to pull her clothes off and make love to her again like she had never experienced before. Being the gentlemen, he is, he allowed her to lead and he followed for now. He did, however, pull her shirt up and gently kissed and rubbed her belly bonding with his future offspring by way of his love for her. He figured he would let her ease into her comfort zone with him then gently grab the reigns and be the head of the relationship as her future husband. He believed in the order God first, man then woman. He knew she believed that order as well.

Since he clearly understood the order, he knew how to be the man and head of the household and not in the sense of overbearing and controlling. He knew it did not mean for her to walk behind him. He valued her place beside him keeping her close and protecting her at all cost even if it meant his life. He'd always known his position as a man. If he did what he was supposed to, he would reap the benefits of her appreciation to him, and she would do what was to be done as the woman of the house.

Mike was a little old fashioned. Growing up, he witnessed his dad as a true God-fearing man. It showed in his interaction with Mike's mother. Finally, he was getting his chance to be with the woman he had on a pedestal and secretly loved the past eight years and be to her what his dad was to his mom. He knew it would not take much to make her happy and promised he would go above the requirements to keep her that way and support her. Morning crept in on them as they slept in the comforts of each other's arms. Blue got up and showered as Mike washed his face and brushed his teeth and left for his house to shower and dress for the day.

The decision was made that she would move into his house and put her place up for sale. She would sleep in one room and he would be in his. They picked out the room they would start decorating for the baby. They wanted to try something different this time around and not make the same stupid mistakes of giving each other privileges and luxuries of getting the marital benefits without officially committing to each other as husband and wife.

This wasn't a typical arrangement, but it was the arrangement they agreed to until they set a wedding date that worked for them. They would begin to date each other on a more serious note and take time to really get to know each other on that level. The expectations were different. Blue called her mother on the way to work and told her about her and Mike's decision.

"Kristen are you sure you know what you are doing?" her mother sighed.

"Yes mommy. I am sure of two things and one is this man loves me and I am in love with him. We won't be shacking per say because I will be in one room and he will be in his. We can make it work mommy I believe in us. This is something different for the both of us and we plan on being married before the baby is born."

"Ok just know what you are doing. I can't make decisions for you. Mike is a wonderful man and I have wanted to see you two together for a long time, so I am excited for you. When do you plan on having a wedding?"

"Well it would not be a big wedding but more like a small ceremony. I am not really wanting a whole bunch of hoopla and I will be in my second or third trimester and showing. I think this is for the best."

"That sounds nice. I am loving that idea because you are like your mama. We are ok with simple."

"Yeah we are, and I just want to keep everything that way. Even if I were not pregnant, I don't want to plan a big extravagant wedding. That money can be used for something better. I have never thought to spend salary money on a wedding people only want to come to see, speculate and may not even bring you a nice gift. A gift at all for that matter. This is not a circus, we are not monkeys therefore you will not be entertainment. I keep my circle small."

"I know. Even growing up it did not take a lot of bells and whistles for you to be happy. Just let me know what I can do to help. Celeste said she already told you when we are coming to help you set up the baby's room when the time comes."

"She told me she needed a niece in her life. She swears this is a girl. But I don't care either way. I really hope my house sales pretty quickly."

"It will. You stay in a very upscale neighborhood. Your home is beautiful. That view is gorgeous."

"Yea Mike's view from his house is better than mine! Since he hasn't been in his house that long and no woman has had the chance stay there to mark it as her territory, we will make it our home. He bought it right after him and the last young lady broke up. His lady friends may have come over for a little food, fun, and entertainment but they couldn't let the sun catch them there sleeping. He was not having it at all. His motto was, *"I don't care what time you come and what we do, you have got to go when we are through!"* When we get married we are going to have to burn both of our beds. We are just going to buy new sets. We can't sleep on those dens of sin as husband and wife."

"Too much information Kristen. I don't want any visuals about either of you."

"My bad. Sorry Ma," Blue smirked.

Blue chuckled to herself. She did feel kind of odd talking about this with her mother, not that she couldn't tell her mother anything, it was just that she had to admit to doing big girl things and it was now out in the open- very out in the open because she is pregnant.

"Ok, I got to go. I have gotten hungry and I have to start packing up this place."

"When are you trying to be out of there?"

"Uuuuuuuum within the next few weeks. I wanna go ahead and get it done. I will start moving some stuff this weekend when I get off work. We are going to hire a moving company. Mike doesn't want me doing too much."

"I understand but call me if you need me," her mother insisted.

"Yes ma'am, but I can manage, besides, you have Big Mama to look out for. I love you."

"I love you too, but still."

They hung up and Blue sat in silence for a few minutes. She took it all in. She was embracing a new and exciting chapter in her life and she began to get excited about it. She never in a million years thought her life would take the turn it had, but she became ok with it. She thought about how loving and supportive her new man and family were. She liked the idea of a man like Michael Long loving her and him being someone she could honestly be herself around. She continued to sit and rubbed her unborn child nestled in the luxuries of her belly. She was so lost in the moment, she found herself with just enough time to rush out the door. She grabbed her belongings and plowed down the street towards work. She was overly irritated on the morning drive to work as people drove as they either had no license or they were newly recipients. One fellow driver caused her to bear down on her horn. His head was down, and his car was drifting. When she passed him, she noticed his fingers were texting away paying no attention to others around him. He sees her and lips, "*Sorry*." She rolled her eyes, threw up her hand, made a left then a right turn and finds herself in her office parking lot.

"Good morning guys," she busted in the door as if someone were behind her.

"Girl you better slow down. What is wrong with you?" Ms. Deb asked peering over her glasses.

"Nothing. It was a crazy ride to work. People driving like idiots this morning, but I am fine," she exhaled.

"Now Kristen you need not be letting folks get your blood pressure up. You have more than just yourself to worry about."

"Yes I know, Ms. Deb which was why I was furious on the ride to work this morning. Those dummies are out there driving crazy with no regards for anyone else. I will be in my office until needed."

She casually walked down the hallway with a sweet smile on her face. She began thinking that in a few months she would be Mrs. Mike Long, and they would be starting a family. As the day passed, she diligently worked as she saw patients and performed the duties of her job. In between time she explored the web in order to start early search for a potential nanny or caregiver for the new bundle of joy.

"Ms. Deeeeeeb come quick please!" Blue summoned her over the intercom.

"What is it child?!" she asks breathing hard propping on the side of the door.

"Why are you out of breath?"

"Because you called me like something was wrong!"

"Oh, I'm sorry. I just wanted to know if you knew if one of the little retired women at church wouldn't mind rocking and spoiling a cute little baby? I am not having any luck right now on this nanny website and so I wanted to know your thoughts on it."

"What website are you on trying to find my baby a caregiver on the internet…. child that is so unholy. You new age parents are out of control."

"Ms. Deb!" she yelped,

"What, I am just being honest. I will make some phone calls when I get home. I thought about retiring so I can spoil this baby."

Ms. Deb flopped down in the chair getting comfortable. She insisted she would keep the new baby until Mike and Blue got situated in all of their new roles. The more she insisted, Blue pushed back assuring her she was a great asset to the practice and could not afford to lose her as a valued player on the team.

Ms. Deb thanked Blue for the compliments and teasingly forewarned her that when it was time for her to officially retire, she was just not going to show up anymore. No sign, no warning. She also warned Blue that if she popped over at her house during work or school hours then she could be found being chased around the house by Mr. Jimmy on his lunch break. Since he was self-employed, that could be anytime.

As they continue to talk, Blue told her of the overwhelming support her mom and sister had given. Blue lets Ms. Deb in on the decorating plans once she gets closer to delivery and how she planned on extending the invitation to his mother so she could feel a part of this as well.

She pleased her with the news of the marriage before the baby was born and how Mike is ready to sign the birth certificate and/or adoption papers if needed to be legally her child's father. Smiling from ear-to-ear Ms. Deb jumped from her chair and did her rendition of her own happy dance as she reiterated what a great man Mike was and reassured her family's support as well. She kissed Blue on the forehead and proceeded to leave the office.

"Thanks again work mom!" she called out.

"Yeeeeeeeees! Get it girl! Yes the baby will call Mike daddy and not Mr. Belton. Mmmmmmmmm well now." she chuckled and closed the door behind her.

Blue laid her head back on her chair and sulked. She rubbed her stomach and began to talk to her unborn child. As she talked, she thought about how scared she was, how parenting was a hard but rewarding job and how she hoped she and Mike could give the baby the tools needed to be a productive citizen of society. Fear consumed her thoughts as she wondered what Mike would say to his family and how they would handle it. She needed them to know she loved Mike, nothing stood in the way of that.

The baby was residue from the love she thought she shared with Big. That relationship was over, and she loved Mike free and clear of Big. She didn't want them to feel she had made a mess of her life and now she wanted him- her best friend to take on someone else's responsibility and fix it. She knew better but her thoughts kept getting the best of her and they were so loud in her head. She feared being with him would destroy his relationship with his parents. She became overwhelmed with the thought of putting more weight than needed on his shoulders. Just as she was about to let out a loud cry, the door opened. Mike walked in. He was carrying large bags of Chinese food. Their eyes connected and they smiled at each other. Ms. Deb came in right behind him.

"Heeeeey beautiful," Mike greeted her.

"Hello my favorite guy," she glowed.

He kissed Blue ever so gently, put the food down, rubbed the baby bump and hugged Ms. Deb. He opened the bags and gave out the lunch he stopped and ordered for the three of them.

"How did you know I was hungry?" she asked as she kissed him again for being an awesome and thoughtful man.

"Who are you kidding? You are always hungry! I can't let you starve out my boy. He will not be born all fragile and frail looking. I need him to come out strong and healthy like his pops, so eat up woman. I'm glad I got here to surprise you both and caught Ms. Deb before she walked out the door."

"Because you know I was on my way to see my Jimmy for a little lunchbreak lovin," Ms. Deb smirked.

Blue's eyes fill with tears. She was grateful that Mike had already responded to the role of dad. She could not image life being any better than what she felt in that moment.

"Hey now why are you crying? What did I do? Why are you so upset? You don't want Chinese? I will run back out and get you something different, just don't cry, Ms. Deb help me out- what did I do?"

"You are a good man Mike Long and the tears you see are tears of gratitude. She loves that you are taking ownership, especially to a baby that was fathered by another man," Ms. Deb explained.

He took Blue in his arms and held her tight. He brought his face to hers and kissed her. He got some Kleenex and wiped her tears and vowed that he would not let go until she flashed that big, beautiful smile that made him fall in love with her each time he saw her. She smiled and he released her from his grip as promised. She slid her hand down his arm into his hand. He squeezed her hand and pulled her close to him.

He was just as hype as she was. He had been waiting to be in her world in this manner from the day he laid eyes on her. He always flexed in the bathroom mirror at home to pump himself up because he had the woman of his dreams and he realized and understood her potential and her love as a mate.

He appreciated that in her he'd found a wife, his good thing and with that yielded favor from the Almighty and he did not take that lightly. He wrapped up the conversation with Blue and Ms. Deb and made Blue aware that he went ahead and called the movers so they could move her big furniture into the extra rooms of the house so that will be done and out of the way. He gave her clear instructions to go home and take a shower, get on a chair or on the bed and relax. Blue graciously accepted her orders. She kissed her future husband and sent him out the door so she could get back to work. The day continued to pass and as they wrapped up the business of the office Blue anticipated going home and doing exactly as she was instructed. They closed the office and Blue hit the road to her man and the first day to a new happiness. Driving home she felt little flutters in her stomach. She smiled as the baby actively moved inside her body for the first time. She could not wait to get home and share that feeling with Mike. She pulled up and he pulled in right behind her.

"Hey again. Will you get the flowers out of the car for me?" she asked.

"Yea baby I got them."

"Oh, guess what? I felt the baby move on the way home tonight!"

"Oooh babe no way. Aww baby that is neat! I can't wait to feel him!" he exclaimed.

"And how do you know this baby is a boy Mr. Long? I mean I am guilty of saying it too, but still."

"I don't know. I just kind of always wanted a son first."

She kissed him, and they continued in the house. He walked into the bathroom and started her a bath. He put a few drops of lavender oil in the bath to help relax her. He laid her towel and robe beside the bathtub. While bathing she smelled the delectable aromas from the kitchen. On the table was her favorite warm cup of cinnamon tea waiting for her. It never mattered the season or the reason. She just liked it.

"How was your bath?" he asked.

"It was great. Thank you," she replied.

"Good, I am glad you enjoyed it."

"I did. Mike I just feel the need to let you know how grateful I am for what you are doing for me-for us. I can't express to you how indebted I am for your love and generosity even as my best friend."

"Baby girl this is how you treat someone you are in love with."

"So, you really hope this is a boy? You hope we have a son?"

"Yea, I would love that. I am happy with whatever God blesses us with. You are even more beautiful to me with this life growing inside you. Your glow is stunning and turning me on."

"Did you really mean what you said about adopting the baby and putting your last name on the birth certificate?" she asked hesitantly.

"Absolutely I am as serious as a heart attack. I meant exactly what I said. I love you and I love this child. He is my best friend's child. It is just that simple Kristen."

"Ok, I will go ahead and see what is needed and start getting the ball rolling on this then."

"Ok sounds good. I know we said we were going to ride down to see my parents. When I called her to tell her we were coming with some news she swore her heart could not take it and she needed to know right then, so I went ahead and told her."

"Oh my God! What did she say?"

"She was happy as crap. She was on the phone crying and slinging snot. Pops in the back yelling my boy! You finally hit that son!"

Blue was floored. She was in aww at how this was all falling together. All of that was easy; it was almost too easy. She just needed to get Big to give up all parental rights so she and Mike could continue to move forward. She sighed as she took in a deep breath and wondered how that part of the puzzle was going to fit. She knew enough to know Big was stubborn and she would have to play her cards just right in order to pull this off.

"You did warn her that the baby is technically not yours. I don't want her looking at the baby trying to figure out why he doesn't look like any of you," she went on.

"Yes, Blue I did-not that it mattered. I explained to them that the baby came before we decided to explore our feelings for each other. They love you as well and they don't care because they know you would never do anything to intentionally hurt me. They want to know I am happy and that makes them happy. To my parents my happiness is all that matters. We have a couple of weeks before Thanksgiving so we will ride down there tomorrow so they can see you us."

She hugged Mike and kissed his chin. On her way to her seat she was stopped by the smells that came from the pots on the stove. Mike shooed her to her seat and fixed her plate.

"What did you cook babe? It smells delicious."

"That is because you are hungry," he laughs.

"Yea if I don't slow down this baby fat is going to be something serious."

"And I will love you in all of your baby fat because I love you."

"Is that so, I love you too," she smiled.

They sat down to dinner. Blue was in food heaven with the smothered chicken in white gravy. Mike had also cooked scalloped potatoes and grilled asparagus. He thought he was a chef in his former life. His mother showed him how to survive in the kitchen, but he had now made cooking a personal trademark. After they ate, they gathered on the couch and cuddle while channel surfing. Blue fell asleep and he watched her peacefully in his arms. He smiled and continued to flip through channels. Before long Mike found himself waking up crouched down on top of Blue's head. Her movement wakes him up.

"Baby girl, he whispered softly in her ear. "Let's go to bed. We have a ride ahead of us tomorrow."

"Ok what time is it?"

"It is eleven: thirty-nine," he said squinting at the clock.

"How long have we been asleep on the couch?"

"A couple of hours. I drifted off holding you. I didn't realize I was that tired until I got still."

"I know right. I always look forward to seeing your parents."

"Once we get up in the morning, we don't have to be in a hurry to get there. We will get breakfast and just take our time riding down."

"Ok that is fine. I love you."

Chapter 2

They gave each other a long kiss goodnight and go off to their rooms. Morning came and Blue woke up and quietly walked around the house. She opened Mike's door and he greeted her with a good morning. He released his bed once he saw she was up and moving around. They showered and dressed for the day. Mike suggested they stay the weekend. Blue obliged him. She loved spending time with his parents. Blue called Mama Bella and told her about her weekend plans. They chatted for a few minutes more, then ended the call. About a half hour into the drive they stopped and got breakfast. They continued their drive until they came to the outlets about twenty miles from his family home. Blue bought several items, and they continued their trip anticipating a fun filled weekend with the first two important people in his life. They pulled in the long driveway and saw his parents standing on the porch.

"Hey mama. Hey old man." Mike calls out.

"Hey son, and hello Kristen. It has been quite a while." Mrs. Long greeted her.

"Hey there pretty darling," Mr. Long smirks.

They greeted each other with lots of hugs and kisses. She always felt very welcomed and loved when she was around the two of them. Pop Long helped Mike with the overnight bag and Mama Long escorted Blue in the house and straight to the kitchen where she had prepared a fabulous brunch for the four of them.

"Oh Mrs. Long everything looks and smells so good," Kristen acknowledged.

"Thank you. I figured Michael made you get up early and had you on that road all day. I was certain when you got here you would want a little snack. I made just a little something for us.

"Thank you Mrs. Long I really appreciate it."

"Please Kristen. I would really love for you to call me mom or something other than Mrs. Long. That was Mr. Long's mama. Besides, we are almost officially family now and I am gaining a daughter I have always wanted."

"Aww thank you, thank you ma for accepting me- us- this situation. I know it was a lot to take in so thank you. You don't have to be so kind and understanding and I appreciate that."

"I will be honest, your situation is not an ideal one, but I must admit you make my son happy. His happiness is all that matters to me. I was a bit worried when I found out, but he assured me that your love was strong for one another and the other man is totally out of the picture. He told me he wanted to adopt this baby. I told him if it is worth it to him, then it is worth it to me and his father. Now that is all that will be said about this situation from here on out. As far as Mama Long is concerned my son has brought his sweet fiancée and their unborn child home to spend time with his parents. Now come on in here and let this baby have some of Granny Long's cooking so he will know who granny is."

Mike and his father walked in the door and witnessed Blue crumble with emotion and tears. She attempted to walk towards Mama Long and tripped. Mike caught her.

"Wait a minute girl. You can't be around here falling. Our insurance frowns upon that and won't cover it!" he teased.

"I am fine. I was getting ready to hug Mama Long and tripped. I can apparently add clumsy to my list of things that happen while pregnant. Waterhead being at the top."

Mike and Pop Long looked at each other and simultaneously blurted out in laughter, "Mama Long?"

"Yes, now who wants to make something of it? She is the daughter you and I could never have Eddie."

Mike's heart skipped two beats. On one hand he felt like a punk for the way he stood and smiled in the midst of the conversation but, on the other hand what and who he prayed for was now in arm's length. He smelled her, touched her, felt her, enjoyed being near her now in ways that seemed so far-fetched a short time ago. He was glad there was a smooth transition from best friend to fiancé. It had been some time since his parents and Blue had been in the same space together but so far the visit confirmed he made the right choice and that Blue truly was the woman for him. They all went in the kitchen enjoyed the meal Mike's mom had prepared for them. After brunch, Mike and Blue cleaned up while his parents rested in the family room off from the kitchen.

They finished the kitchen and Mike took Blue for a walk around his old neighborhood. About an hour into their walk it began to get cool, since neither had a jacket, they hurriedly walked back to the house. Mike noticed a few extra cars in the driveway. He and Blue eased into the door with caution. Mike had no idea who the cars belong to. He was going to keep it safe and tread lightly just in case it was some of the old church ladies who still like to pinch his cheeks like they did when he was a child. He opened the door and walked into a house full of family. His parents had called their sisters and brother and his cousins. Mike and Blue were swarmed by the greetings of hellos with hugs and kisses that awaited them in the family room of his old house. He could not believe it. He had not seen his extended family in a very long time. None of them had met Blue. His parents decided to make that happen.

To celebrate the new engagement, the families loaded up and went to Mike's favorite restaurant. It was a little buffet place with a southern style feel of comfort to it. The Longs and their extended family laughed and joked over dinner. Tears of laughter and joy flooded the table as they all reminisced about the past. They laughed at the present and made new promises for the future. Blue felt right at home amongst her official new family. The younger girls volunteered to babysit when they came to visit. The older women promised to show her how to really have a good time once she'd given birth. His parents were pleased to announce to the world or at least to all that were listening in the restaurant, that they had an unsurmountable joy knowing their son and the woman of his dreams had finally come to their senses and made the necessary provisions to spend the rest of their lives together. It was a night that none of them especially Blue would ever forget.

"Oh my God Mike. I am so in love with your family. I feel so welcomed. Do you think they know?" she whispered.

"Uuumm know what?" he whispered confused.

"About our situation?" she whispered.

"Uuuuummmmm what about our situation, and why are we whispering?"

"About the baby not really being yours?"

"What!? First off that is none of their business and second who the hell gone tell them and third why does that matter?! All anybody needs to know is that we are in love, happy as hell, and going to spend the rest of our lives together as a family. It really is as simple as how everyone sees us right now. The baby situation is null and void. The only thing that matters is that especially in the eyes of outsiders we are engaged, you are having my baby and I am extremely in love with you as are you with me." he frustratedly cleared his throat.

"You're right that doesn't matter. The only people it matters to is you and me."

"And knowing that tidbit of information, baby please don't bring that up again. You are going to drive yourself crazy. If I am ok, you should be. We really must move past that. Look around Blue, whether they know or not, nobody cares," he assured.

"I know and you're right. I'm sorry," she said scanning the smiling faces of his family.

"Are you finished eating. Come on let's get you back to the house and chill."

They broke from their sidebar conversation and noticed the late hours of the evening hurried upon them. They finish with dinner. Mike asked for the ticket from the waiter but Pop Long took it from him and paid the bill. They hugged and kissed in massive amounts and left each other with kind parting words and farewell wishes until they met again. They collected his parents and went back to the house. They continued the laugh and fellowship on the drive home.

"So Kristen, when is that sweet little grandbaby of ours going to be born?" Mama Long peeped her head between the seats and asked.

"My expected due date is March 17th."

"Mike that is daddy's birthday. He would have been 100 years old had he live to see it this past March."

"Oh woow. How old was he when he died?" Blue asked.

"He was 43. Mike never knew him. He died long before Michael was thought about. Matter of fact, you are his namesake."

"Oh ok." Mike noted.

"Kristen have you given any thoughts to the naming of the baby yet?" Mama Long inquired.

"I haven't gotten any farther than Kristopher Michael Long if it is a boy." she smiled.

Mike reached over and put his hand on hers. He was smitten with the fact she was to allow the baby to carry on his name. He wanted to pull the car over and tongue her down to show his appreciation for her right there on the side of the road. Since his parents were in the back, he hesitantly kept driving and winked at her instead. They arrived at the house and go inside. It is 8:45 and for his parents that was late. Mike convinced his parents to stay up a few more hours and they continued to talk about the events of the day. Shortly afterward everyone headed off to their perspective sleeping quarters.

"Maaaaaaaaa! Where is my favorite blanket?" he whined.

"I put it on the couch already. I don't know why you like sleeping on that couch with that old blanket especially when there's a perfectly good bed in your old room."

"Oh ok, I didn't see it. That old couch is comfortable. I love you good night ma."

"Good night son, love you more."

He walked to the doorway of the guest room and kissed the future Mrs. Long goodnight. He looked back at her as he walked the long hall to the family room and bunkered down on the couch. Fiancée or not, there would be no shared sleeping quarters out of respect for his parents' space. In their house it did not matter he and Blue were making plans to be Mr. and Mrs. Until it was official there would never be any sharing of the beds there. The next morning, they hung around the house and ate passing the day away. In between meals, Mike spent time with his dad cleaning and making small repairs. Blue spent time with Mama Long going through some of Mike's baby belongings. She and Blue talk about how Mike was as a child and how he was such a good son. She gave Mama Long an invitation to come up with the rest of the ladies for the room decorating party.

When they finished they reconvened to the family room and looked at old photo albums and home videos. Before long, it was bedtime. They said their goodnight's and went to their rooms. Morning came. Blue and Mike get up and get dressed. Mike packed the car. They kissed and hugged and thanked his parents for their hospitality. They took the scenic route on the drive back home in the same leisurely manner they came. They stopped at another outlet and spent a few hours there. Their affection showed so sweetly on each other that many people smiled as they walked by. They held hands, kissed, took selfies, and really enjoyed each other on their outing. They shopped and looked at baby items to get some ideas of what kinds of baby gadgets were out. They agreed to purchase a few unisex pieces for baby Long.

"Glad we don't have to buy much of this stuff. Leesi has everything we need for whatever we are having. So her, mama and Ms. Deb are going to come and do whatever they want to the room we picked out as the baby's room once we find out the sex. I also told your mother, so hopefully we will see your parents that weekend as well. It was made clear to me that on that day, I need to get missing and stay out of the way. They told me to apologize to you for them in advance."

"Apology accepted. Do I get to get out of the way and sit down somewhere?" he begged.

"Yeah probably after you fellas put together and shift furniture. I am gonna love having everyone under the same roof. I hope your parents come. It is going to be awesome. I am excited already!"

"I'm sure they will baby. This is right up mama's alley."

He grabbed her from behind and pulled her close to him. She leaned in and fit her body into his. He put his hand on her belly and rubbed, he felt the baby kick. They looked at each other and smiled. The moment was priceless, and in a little under six months, they would meet their little person face to face. Mike was in love, not just with her, but with the life he'd been blessed with. He'd promised God to love Blue and the baby as his own and now it had become surreal. As they stood on the sidewalk Mike kneeled down and talked to the baby.

The more he talked, the more the baby kicked and moved in response to his voice. Almost twenty minutes had gone by as they stood on the sidewalk and Mike got acquainted with their unborn child. Blue even video recorded it from her view. It was a moment for the baby book. They finished shopping and voyaged nonchalantly home. They pulled in the garage and went in the house. Blue went straight for the shower and her pajamas. She came back to the kitchen and helped Mike put away the food his mother sent back with them. She had eaten herself five pounds heavier according to the scales and enjoyed every minute of it. She was lost in a happiness that she had prayed and dreamed about for quite some time.

"I was thinking lady love, why don't we have Christmas at our home? Why not invite all our friends and family here to celebrate our first Christmas together?"

"Oh, that sounds perfect. Where will we spend Thanksgiving?"

"With your mother of course since we just saw my parents. It is only fair. Don't you think?"

"Babe I love the idea. If that is what you wanna do," she concurred.

"Well it is. I figure we can have Christmas dinner at the lounge and that way you don't have to clean up the house or cook. I can have it all done there. We can decorate and do the whole nine yards and then come back home."

"I love you. I should have listened a long time ago, and life would have been so much easier. I can't remember being this happy before you and I don't want to imagine life without you. Umm will I get the same special treatment if we have baby number two?"

"Nawl girl you will be a professional by then. It won't be an if but when. I told you my folks got to have some grandkids to leave that bingo money to," he laughed.

"Ha-ha ha ha ha you are too funny."

"You are laughing, but my parents aren't playing," he warned trying to keep a straight face.

They kissed and went off to bed. Morning greeted her with the excitement of finding out the sex of the baby. She and Mike left her appointment hoping to come out with exciting news to share. Instead they were saddened with the uncooperative spirit that dwelled in the little person taking up space in her body. They were told if there was more cooperation on the baby's end then the sex could be determined at the next visit. After her appointment Mike met a general contractor at the meeting place of his newest business. Once they confirmed the sex of the baby, he could have the name sign made and put it on the building.

Mike's gut urged him that the baby was a boy. He only found it befitting to name the building after their first born- Kristopher's. He just needed to confirm. The name of the space would still be a secret to Blue. He wanted to surprise her once the name was on the outside of the building and bring her down to see it. The new spot was to be open by mid-December. He knew that with the stress of the lounge and with preparation for the baby, things were going to be slightly strained and hectic around their house. However, it all had to be done. He had his game plan. He just had to make sure he could cxccutc it. Thc ncxt day thcy both got up and went to their places of work. Over the next several days Blue stopped by her place after work. She and Ms. Deb packed up some more of her things. She packed up a lot of unwanted items and sent them to a homeless shelter.

"I didn't know one person could have so much stuff. My Lord chile, what is all of this? Wait Kristen didn't I give you this a few years back? Why is it tucked down in the closet?"

"Well, ummm see what had happened was I forgot I stuck it down in there. Yea that's it," she stuttered.

"I guess you not keeping it?" Ms. Deb asked.

"OOOOOh no ma'am! I thank you for it, but I think someone else can get better use of it than I. I have used all the other gifts you have given me though. What were you thinking with that one?"

"Ha, really? I was trying to do different that year. Looking at it, I too could ask myself what was I thinking?"

"Ms. Deb you did waaaaay different. I tried to like it, but I couldn't, sorry!"

"Really? Woooow," she laughed. "Do you have any more boxes? This one is full. Chile where are you gonna put all of this stuff?"

"Yea, Mike put some in the third bedroom. Uuuuuuh I don't know. We have not discussed it yet. We can put my chairs in the loft upstairs on the third level and make it the entertainment area. He has already taken my bedroom furniture for me to sleep on in my room. Once we get married, we will replace our old bedroom furniture. Just can't be sleeping on those fornicated out mattresses! That is not Godly going into a marriage. There is the baby's room downstairs with ours and then there are two extra rooms upstairs on the second level."

"That sounds like a lot of house and that is T-M-I!"

"Oops, my bad. It is. He has someone come in and clean especially the downstairs area twice a week because he is never home and doesn't have time."

"So, are you all going to keep the housekeeper?"

"If she's ugly!" she laughed. No but seriously, I guess for now. At least until I can get a feel for keeping up that big house. That is a lot along with being a new mom, wife and employed full time."

"You are a mess! Ms. Deb laughed. "Better believe it honey, your hands will be full, but you can do it. You have a good support system and that is going to help out a lot."

Mr. Jim announced himself as he opened the door and followed their voices through the house. The ladies were coming from the back bedroom with boxes when he followed them in the master bathroom to clean out the cabinets. He rolled his sleeves up and fell in place to help.

"How's it going baby girl?" Mr. Jim asked Blue.

"I am so excited about life and love right now Mr. Jim!"

"That is wonderful. Glad to see what we all have been praying for finally happened. You both are good kids, and I knew that true happiness would never come for either of you until you experienced it with each other. God answers prayers!"

"Preach baby!" Ms. Deb yelled as she waved a hand.

"Yea but look at the mess that was made right before."

"Honey don't you know that was all a part of God's plan. He will permit some things to be so in order to get you where He needs you to be. The good, bad and the ugly work to help you fulfil His greater purpose for you."

"I am getting my share of it all-especially the bad," she grunted.

"Ya know even in your mistakes, God loves you and He knows you love Him. You and Mike where purposed so that the two of you could become one flesh. I noticed you have missed a couple of Sundays are you ok?"

"Yea. Just dealing with this move and all. We went to see his parents this past weekend. We will get back on it. Prayerfully this Sunday."

"Ok afterwards you and Mike can come to the house for Sunday dinner," Ms. Deb spoke up.

"Ok Ms. Deb. I will let him know. I am sure he won't mind," Blue assured.

"Won't mind what?" Mike walks through the door. Looking around to see what else needed to be done to complete the move."

"Hey baby. What are you doing here?" Blue asked surprised.

"I just came to make sure you have not been over doing it," Mike said raising his eyebrow at her.

"No, I haven't. Ms. Deb just invited us to dinner Sunday after church."

"Oh, ok cool. Ms. Deb you know I don't mind your cooking at all. Do we need to bring anything?" Mike asked.

"No baby just your precious little self and an empty stomach!"

"Well, now I can do that. We need to let Kristen get in the kitchen with you. I'm just saying. Mama Bella said she could cook. She been feeding me take out for eight years. One thing is for sure, love never happened because of a meal I tell you that!"

"So what are you saying Mr. Long? I cook- I mean I can cook. I just don't," Blue stammered.

"Yea, well you might need to step up your pots and pan game Missy because you are getting ready to have a family and we are going to have to eat," Mike suggested.

"I think I am going to go into the other room and start packing. It's becoming a little thick in here," Blue sashayed off.

They all laughed at her as she walked away. She turned around and gave them her best stare down. Mike left and went back to work. Mr. Jim left the ladies and went into another room and continued to pack boxes. They worked a few more hours, got to a stopping point and went home. It was ten o'clock and Blue was pulling in the garage. Mike left a light on for her and a light snack with a note attached. *"Bae don't wait up. I will be a while at the lounge. I love you and will see you in the morning. I am not going to wake you. Lock up."* Blue followed Mike's instructions. She found some of her things a new home in the house. She ate her snack, showered then went off to bed. She felt somewhat uneasy sleeping in her bed without Mike being in the house. Blue wasn't used to the living arrangements. She felt way out of her element being in that big house by herself.

She grabbed her pillow and found herself in the middle of Mike's bed. Unexpecting to see her in his bed he flipped the light on then quickly back off hoping not to wake her. He grabbed his pajamas and went to the bathroom. He showered then joined her in bed. He gently slid her legs over. She felt him and woke up long enough to greet him. She adjusted herself accordingly to let him in the bed then she slid back over and nestled her body in the comforts of his. Morning came and she gently kissed him and eased her way from under him. She dressed for work and on her way out of the door, her phone rang. It was Big.

"The sun hasn't been up long enough for foolishness. What in God's name do you want? Why are you calling me? Are you serious right now?" she whispered running out of the house without being heard.

"Dang girl. Good morning to you too. I just wanted to see how you were doing. You still talking about you pregnant?"

"You have no need to worry or wonder about me or this baby. I was going to call you and ask if you and I could meet to discuss some things, but since foolishness is still your middle name and being simple is your game, I am however glad you called because the last time we saw each other you put your hands on me and we aren't giving you the space to do that again. Look, I need you to sign over your parental rights as the father of this child. We want absolutely nothing to do with you---EVER! Please don't make this any hard. Let's just act like adults and handle this please."

"I ain't signing over nothing because that little bastard is not mine! You know it. I don't know why you think I am going to admit to this being my baby. You just like all the rest of them. You just want to be paid, but YOU WILL NOT GET CHILD SUPPORT. YOU WILL NOT GET ANOTHER DIME FROM ME. I PLAYED THAT GAME WITH THE HOUSE. I WON'T DO IT WITH THIS KID. YOU TURN TO GOOD OLE MIKE FOR EVERYTHING ELSE. LET HIM RAISE IT. THAT WOULD BE RIGHT UP HIS ALLEY. HELL, HE WOULD SHOVEL SHIT IF IT MEANT BEING CLOSE TO YOU!" he shouted.

"Look I don't need this kind of stress. I am on my way to work. If you don't agree to sign over your rights, there is more than one way to handle this. Terrance please hear me when I tell you DON'T CALL ME EVER AGAIN. We don't want anything to do with you!"

She hung up on him-upset to the point of shaking. The harder the tears feel the more knots and pain she felt in her stomach. She had never felt that feeling before. She took deep breaths to try and calm herself. She pulled up at the office and saw Ms. Deb in the parking lot.

"What is wrong? I saw it all over your face when you pulled in?" Ms. Deb inquired.

"Terrance called me this morning."

"For what?"

"My question exactly. I told him I wanted him to give up all his parental rights and he is insisting he doesn't have any because the "lil bastard" ain't his. His words, not mine."

"Kristen what the…...? That punk! Did you tell him you moved on and that you have a real man now?"

"Sure I didn't. That is none of his business! He doesn't need to be concerned with anything other than this child and that is no longer his worry."

"Are you going to tell Mike?"

"Nope and neither are you! I am serious. Mike doesn't need to be worried with this silliness. I can handle Terrance. His bark is worse than his bite. He said some very nasty things on that phone. He is getting to a point of no return. He denies the baby and I am ok with that. Mike and I will be married by the time the baby comes. Mike's name will be on the birth certificate. I was just trying to give him a courtesy since he is the sperm donor. He now will be treated as a stranger and handled accordingly. I can always say I don't know who the biological father is and since he doesn't know my where abouts then how will he know what I did. Mike can go ahead and sign the adoption papers as well, so God forbid something happens to me, he can't try and be stupid and take this baby from him."

"I know you are a smart young lady. Didn't see that side of you coming but you gotta handle your business if you say you got this, I won't say anything else but make sure you have tried all the right ways first."

"Thank you. I know I will," she mumbles. "Terrance only acts crazy. He loves his freedom of playing ball so he's not trying to go to jail."

"Ok if you say so."

Chapter 3

They continue to talk in between Blue seeing her patients. She could not believe how Big tried to handle her this morning over the phone. She tried to shake it, but it still nudged at her feelings a little.

"On my lunch today, I will go and find out the sex of the baby. I am so excited. I'm ready for you guys to put this child's room together. Hope the cooperation is better today than last time," Blue announced.

"Yea, I want to be on a mission to start buying stuff, but I don't know what to buy. I haven't had to buy baby clothes in so long. I am sure things have changed since then. What kind of baby items are out now?" Ms. Deb inquired.

"Don't buy anything yet. Hold your horses. The different stuff out there for babies could fill the hole in the Grand Canyon," Blue warned.

"Ok but I will let them run loose after you tell me today what we are having," Ms. Deb insisted.

"That is fair enough! But still don't go crazy. I will still have a baby shower. Celeste is bringing a lot of her kids' baby items and other baby items will be gifted to me. Dern it is almost 10:30. This morning is flying by. I need to call Mike and see if he will be able to go with me to this appointment. I know he has other stuff he can do."

"You know he will make time, and you sound crazy to think that man is going to miss his best friend's/fiancée/baby mama to be appointment that is going to reveal the sex of his unborn child. Kristen slap yourself. I mean really."

"Dang Ms. Deb you just be putting it out there. Glad I am not sensitive."

"No need to be. It is what it is. You are planning a life and family with this man. He can't tell you or show you any clearer that he is in it for the long haul. Stop the second guessing and just be happy and enjoy this. Let this be my last time saying it."

"Ok yes ma'am. It won't happen again. I need to go ahead and call Mike while I am thinking about it and remind him."

Blue stepped in her office and called Mike to remind him about the appointment. He told her he would come pick her up from the office and take her to the appointment then drop her back off at work. Mike arrived a few minutes early. He called Blue to let her know he was in the parking lot. She came out smiling and eager to see him. They kissed and made their way to the doctor's office.

"Hey bae. How was your morning? You can make a right here and then a left at the next street. It is that big building on the right."

"It was good, I was still asleep when you called. I heard your phone this morning-was everything ok?

"Yes yes," she stammered. I can't wait to find out the sex of this baby. Are you ready to see all of the ladies and their bellies? I don't know why you get so squeamish. You look and play with mine," she said getting out of the car.

"Yea, I guess it was the initial shock of it all with seeing all pregnant women up close and personal.

Everything your body endures to bring life into this world is amazing. It's really a beautiful thing. I promise I am good." he assured opening the door.

"Aww bae. We are going in this door right here and getting on the elevators to the second floor. It is the first door here on the left."

Blue checked in for her appointment then sat down beside Mike. He looked around attentively and heard different pieces of conversation around the room. There were older woman, younger women, women there with their assumed significant others and some were alone. There was a mom with her daughter and both of them due in months of each other. Ladies from all sects and walks of life. He paid close attention to the sign that showcased every service the office offered these different women. From invitro fertilization to birth control. Pamphlets from adoption and surrogate pregnancies, on how to cope with miscarriage or abortion. He respected what women went through as their bodies changed to become mothers, but he found himself with a new appreciation for them. He was even more appreciative that God gave the child birthing task to women and not men and he was thankful to be a man. One woman began to have contractions sitting in the lobby. Blue looked over and grabbed Mike's hand resting it on his leg to calm his nerves.

"Ms. Stancil," the nurse called her back.

They followed the nurse to the back. Mike waited in the seating area she appointed him to. A few minutes later, he was summoned to join Blue. Blue laid on the table reaching for Mike's hand and had very small talk while they waited. The door opened and they are greeted.

Within minutes the lights go off and Blue scoots down to the edge of the table and the wand was inserted. Blue squeezed Mike's hand. The baby appeared on the screen. The heartbeat and movement was strong.

"Listen to that strong heartbeat Mike!"

"Yeah baby I hear it. Will you be able to tell us the sex of the baby?"

"I will if this little active one cooperates." she said clicking away at the screen. "Let me see, ok here we go. Alright now let's see if you all are the proud parents of a boy or girl. Come on little friend." she pleaded moving the wand for the perfect picture, "It-is-aaaa-BOY!" she announced.

"Oh my God! Mike we are having a boy! Look at him."

"I see baby. I love you. We are going to be into baseball."

"Aww baby. I love you Mike Long. Look at our baby. Kristopher Michael Long. He's perfect!

Blue felt the tears stream down her face. She pulled herself together and dressed. It was all coming together, and it could not have been better. Mike leaned down and kissed her belly and told his son hello. She pulled her shirt down and met the doctor in a different room. She got undressed again from the bottoms down and put a sheet across her lap. Minutes later the doctor comes in and they have conversation. They talk about the baby and how things had been with the pregnancy. While they talk the doctor is examining Blue and the baby. Michael sat there as another object found its way into his girl. The doctor inserted her first two fingers in Blue to examine her uterus and make sure everything is set and aligned as it should be.

"Ok lady everything looks good. Your measurements are aligning. You are a little over five months and your due date we are still confirming on March 17th. You are right on target. We will see you in a month and the closer you get we will see you more frequent. You all have a good one and enjoy Thanksgiving."

"Thanks doc, you as well."

They proceeded to check out. She scheduled her next appointment and left the office excited and more in love with the son growing in her womb. Mike held the door for her as she walked through. They continued to bask in the great news.

"Well that was interesting. I felt violated for you with the wands and the fingers. I am happy to be a man. Is this what is to be expected each time? I thought I was ready; I need a little more time."

"When you are having a baby, honey discretion goes out the window. So just be ready because almost every doctor's appointment you are going to see my vagina whether you like or not."

"Oh I like it just NOT like that. I want to be inside you like that girl! That wand is lucky. I'm jealous," he joked.

"What did you say? Boy I heard you! Trust me future husband soon enough you will be able to get all of me you can handle."

"Lawd I can't wait. Man, to fully experience you as my wife. The marriage bed is undefiled, and boy is it going to be on. Do you want to go home and practice?" Mike wondered.

"Yea that sample was nice. I can only imagine what it will be like when we have no restraints. Dude as tempting as that sounds I shall pass. I have to go back to work and remember our agreement."

"Yea I know but that glow is making me want you even more. Mmmm you are making my man part stand at attention!"

"You will have your chance to have all of me and unless you plan on calling "Palmetta" then I suggest you stand at ease my good sir."

"Zip your jacket up and get out of my car. It is cool out there. I can't have you getting sick."

The chill of the autumn air greeted her opened door. She leaned over and kissed him. November was in the air all around the car, but inside was a hot summer night. Kissing him sparked an arousal in her body. She had to talk herself out of taking him right there. He grabbed her face and leaned in closer kissing her more intently. He put her hand on his man part to let her feel the effect of her on him. She smiled at him sweetly.

"See girl you are about to start something we can't finish, now gone and get out. You let all of the heat out of the car. It is cold in here now," he said turning up the heat and rubbing his hands together.

"Whatever black boy. Are you going to be home when I get there or are you going over to the lounge now? I planned on making dinner tonight. I wanted to surprise you, but I know you want or need to work late night some nights and I didn't want the surprise to be on me when you didn't come home until later than anticipated." she said.

"I will be home by before you get there. I have a few errands to run and then I am going back to the house. I'll lay down until you get there or until it is time to eat. I am leaving about nine. This weekend we have four parties and a banquet. I have to tie up a few loose ends with each event."

"Ok well I got to get back in here," she insisted.

"Did you eat anything?"

"Yea I packed a salad."

"Ok as long as you have something."

"Yes sir. See ya tonight."

She closed the car door and unlocked the front door to her practice. Standing on the doorstep Ms. Deb awaited the news.

"Sooo what are we having?"

"Lord Ms. Deb let me catch just a little bit of my breath. Wheeew! We are having a Kristopher Michael Long!" Blue exclaimed.

"My word child that is fantastic! I love his name. It is so promising. Thank you."

"No problem. I am glad you like it," she chuckled. "I guess I will call my family tonight and let them know the sex of the baby. Oh man Celeste is going to be hot. Glad she didn't make any bets. She would have surely lost. She just knew this was a girl. Oh, I need to check on Monica. She gives birth to my Godchild next month. She's having the girl. She doesn't even know I am pregnant. But hey, neither did I for the first four months. Aww man, this baby needs godparents! When I first found out, Mike was drafted for position of godfather, but since his roll has changed, I hadn't really had time to think about it with all that has been going on. I guess Mike and I will talk about it and discuss it more when the time gets closer," she panicked.

"Doc, I need you to breathe!" Ms. Deb insisted.

"Changing the subject a bit, Mr. Tomas is a great asset around here."

"Yea I know. He and I talked about him being a full partner here at the beginning of the year since he will be finishing his internship next month." she agreed taking in slow breaths.

"That will be nice. It would definitely take some of the work load off you and allow for opportunity to expand the clientele."

"Right because he would have his clients and I would have mine. But sadly, Ms. Deb, I really don't know how long I want to be out on maternity leave with my baby. I know I have a business to run and all. I really want to be out longer than six or eight weeks. I am truly thinking hard about staying home for a while and take it all in. Yes, I know I would be a fool to leave my business when it is flourishing. I am a high commodity but so is my baby. I wanna enjoy him."

"I totally understand how you feel. God afforded me that with the kids. We agreed when Jenna was born that no matter how many followed after her- I would not even entertain the idea of looking for work until the last child got into kindergarten. I really didn't get serious about a job until I saw this one. That is my story, you have to do what you think is best for your family."

"Yea I know. You made it clear in your interview that you were not hard up for a job."

They continued to see patients one after the other. Her afternoon was swamped. Blue couldn't see anything past making it home and taking a long hot shower and mustering up enough strength to cook Mike the fabulous meal she had promised. At the close of the day she locked up the office and thanked her staff for a great day. She hurried off and quickly ran to the grocery store and picked up the items needed for dinner. She didn't have time to check inventory at the house before she left so she bought everything she thought she may have needed. Anything extra would grace the pantry shelf. She drove down the highway a little faster than normal. She'd been known to drive as fast as needed and she felt this was one of those moments. Mike heard the garage open. He cut on some lights and opened the door for her.

"Hey. I thought you were still lying down?"

"I was laying down. I was in the middle of turning over when I heard the garage door open. I went ahead and jumped up because I knew it was dark in here and I hadn't turned any lights on."

"Thanks babe," she said looking at the clock. "I was speeding down the highway thinking it was way later than what it is. It is November and I still have not adjusted to falling back with this time."

"No problem. What all did you buy? Like do you have the kitchen sink in these bags too?"

"No, I don't. I just picked up dinner and I picked up some extra stuff for the house. It is only four bags."

"These bags are heavy. Was there a four-bag minimum?"

"Michael! Go sit yourself down so I can start cooking. On second thought I am going to prep everything first, take my shower and then cook. That way if you want me for dessert, I am already prepared. Otherwise, I will have you fed and burped in an hour.

"I hear you Chef Ann."

"Don't hate Mike. I told you I can cook. I just never really had to."

"We shall see. I know you have never had to cook. For as long as we have known each other you have been eating out. Some nights you have come over and ransacked my fridge. Come to think of it, I might want to pray before and after a meal. I have NEVER seen you in front of a stove not even to heat up your food."

"Really Mike? How you just going to try and play my face like that?"

"Bae, I love you, but I am a little scared right now."

"If you don't get out of this kitchen and go lay down boooooooy!"

"Ok I am going!"

He went into his room laughing uncontrollably. Blue's hair stood up on the back of her neck. She knew Mike was only playing but still her hormones were about to get the best of her. She sucked up her emotions and headed for the shower. After she showered, she went into the kitchen and began to create her masterpiece. The mushrooms were sautéing and noodles boiling while she cut up other fresh vegetables. The aromas coming from the kitchen gave Mike a little confidence that she might have known what she was doing.

"Giiirl what are you doing in here? You have it smelling good!"

"Go sit down! Yes I know and thank you," she said sticking out her tongue.

"Nope come here."

He pulled her close and kissed her. She relaxed her body in his arms. They kiss again. He leaned down pulled up her shirt and began to kiss her neck. He ran his hands across Blue's stomach saying a quick hello to the unborn child. He was fascinated with how the baby responded to him even from inside the womb. He kissed her stomach then kissed her again. He softly kissed and rubbed her shoulders. They breathe heavily fighting the urge to move toward somebody's bedroom. Blue heard the pot start to boil over. Without thinking she ran over and reached for it with no mitt and burned herself.

"Oooooww! Dang it fire," she muffled.

"You're sticking your hands to hot pots now? Let me take a look at it.

"Yep! That is what I do. I'm fine it's not that bad. It is not blistered or anything. I barely touched it honestly. It is fine. I will just run some cold water over it."

"I know, I just want to check it out."

He looked her over attentively. Her heart fluttered watching him make a fuss over just a small burn. She had been around Mike and his other girlfriends and it was nothing like this. As his best friend she noted he cared but she knew this was different and she liked the fact that she received better attention and treatment than the other ladies that had come before her. He finished tending to her hand and moved out of her way allowing her to finish dinner.

"Baby, are you ready to eat? I baked a small duck with a mushroom gravy on a bed of rice. I have macaroni and cheese and there is fresh corn on the cob. You also have a choice of mixed greens or a salad. There are also fresh baked rolls. I didn't know if you had any of your beer in the fridge, so I bought you some. I put one in the freezer so it would be nice and cold for you to drink with dinner."

"Are you sure you cooked that?" he asked lingering around the pots. Everything looks delicious. Do it Chef Kris. I hope it taste good. Girl if that gravy is good, I'm gonna sit it by the bed and we can aaa…" he winked.

"Why are you so silly, you are such a romantic cornball. Did you put food condiments beside the bed for any other girlfriend?"

"Uh no because my mama told me not to play with my food-now! But I might make an exception with you. Where did that question come from? That was random." he said slightly confused as he scratched his head.

"Oh nowhere, guess I fell back into best friend mode, although I must say, I have never seen you so attentive to any other woman."

"The rest of those women weren't you. I mean at all times I treated them with high regards, but I couldn't treat them better than the woman I patiently waited on to come to her senses. Now that she has, doing what I do is easy and second nature."

Blue swallowed hard and looked away smiling. Even as her friend Mike had always known how to appeal to that side of her. She handed him his beer from the freezer followed by a kiss. She fixed their plates and he grabbed eating utensils and napkins. Blue sat down and Mike blessed the food, and they ate. He said another silent prayer in his head hoping the food would be good and took a bite. She'd pleasantly surprised him with the meal.

"Babe, this food is great. I can't believe that in eight almost nine years you have had these kind of cooking skills under your belt. You keep cooking like that, and I may let you do it more often. I can't wait to see how you cook in the bedroom after we are married."

"I told you I could cook. I know my way around the kitchen." she bragged. "Lucky for you bruh, I know what I am doing in that area as well. Wait until we are married. I got something for you. Lord I got a whole lot of something for you. When I have this baby, you are really going to be in trouble!"

"Ooooooo hurt me girl. Lawd have mercy! Don't threaten me with a good time!" he teased.

"You are a mess. Finish your dinner so you can lay back down. You are going to be up all night. I won't see you until in the morning. I may be gone by the time you get in."

"No baby I am definitely trying to finish up tonight so I can be here to kiss you good morning. I want to be the last thing you see and feel when you leave home. I know you are the first thing I want to see when I get here. Thank you baby!"

"Aww you are too good to me. What are you thanking me for?"

"You haven't seen anything yet and for making this house finally begin to feel like a home. You're nice to come home to," he said rubbing her shoulder.

"I believe I haven't seen the best of you-of us. Lover we are just getting started. The best is yet to come. I love you Michael Edward Long!"

"Aawww girl!"

They finished dinner. Blue cleared the table and put away the food. Mike insisted she let him help. After a few rounds of back-and-forth, Mike finally conceded and laid down. Between being on her feet at work all day and standing in the kitchen cooking and cleaning she was tired. To her it was well worth it especially since Mike appreciated it. She laid across Mike's bed until it was time for him to get ready for work.

"Baby, dinner was delicious. I know you are worn out."

"Thank you. I am just a little tired. Baby boy has me hurting all down in my back."

"Turn on your side," Mike suggested moving towards her.

She slid over on her bed and makes room for him. She leaned over to her side and Mike began to rub her back and feet. She wiggled her toes enjoying the touch and kisses he provided. He slid up behind her and wrapped her deep in his arms and held her as tight as he could. She nestled closely into him. They laid in the security of each other in the silence. Their bodies continued to learn each other's language as they conformed to each other in complete harmony. He rubbed her stomach and they dozed off. Blue turned over looked at the clock and jumped waking Mike.

"Hey-hey, what is wrong, why are you jumping?" he stammered.

"What time did you have to leave? It is almost nine o'clock."

"I told them I would be there about nine thirty. Shoot," he sighed. "Dang you feel so good. Let me go ahead and get up and get myself together so I can leave. Are you going to be straight while I am gone? I just don't like to leave you here by yourself."

"Yes baby I will be fine. If I get too lonely then I know my way to the lounge or to Ms. Deb's, but I promise I will be ok. Mike I am a big girl. Before you I lived by myself. I adjust well."

"Yea I know it just seems a little different now. I feel like I need to be here with you, since I don't really get to see you during the day. I just need to make sure you're straight. This is what I am supposed to do."

"Like really, have you always been like this?"

"Yes, it just wasn't your time to see it. This man has always been here patiently waiting on you. Honestly, my boys were like man let that dream die. It is never happening. I knew time would permit itself and here we are. You couldn't see past us being friends, but I had us married and in our happily ever after from the first time we said hello."

Blue pulled him to her and kissed him repeatedly. She constantly saw how deep his love went for her and how patiently he was in waiting. She loved that as freely as he gave his love, he could accept hers. She knew she was worth it. It seemed as if she had spent much of her dating years in loser city. She had almost forgotten the qualities she prayed for in her soulmate or as she liked to call him her rib giver. Now that it had slapped her in the face, she adored taking it all in.

She couldn't believe his friends would tell him to let go of the dream of them. Although she could put herself in his shoes, seeing as she was recently connected to a man that seemingly absolutely had no desire to have a life with her outside the bedroom. The only difference between her and Big was she was willing to yield to the love Mike gave. Unlike Big who instead continued to run and not deal with his own demons. Demons that caused him to make excuses and not want to commit to anyone or anything but the fast life that included cheap tricks and football. Looking back, she didn't know what made her any different from the other females he dealt with. She thought maybe she wasn't any different at all.

She would have like to believe she was different but wasn't sure she was. Then she remembered it was the challenge that made Big want to conquer her time and attention. She was so busy entertaining him, she missed the signs of him picking up a new toy. She was glad her dating path led her to Mike and the assured happiness they had to offer each other. She knew what he gave was genuine and she was truly willing to accept it and reciprocate that love even more in return to him. He put his shoes on. He threw his clothes in the basket and Blue walked him to the door and kissed him goodnight. She locked the door and set the alarm. Her phone rang.

"Hey Leesi, I was just about to call you. We found out the sex of the baby today. We are having a boy!"

"Ahh Kris! How did you let me down like that? I forgive you though and you can make it up to me by having me a little girl."

"You are so silly. Let me see if I can handle this little guy. Mike does want at least two more children though. He doesn't care the sex. His parents just need to have somebody to leave their bingo money to."

"Why are you stuuupid?" Celeste giggles.

"What?! Mike says that foolishness all the time," she laughs.

"Have you at least given my little milk dud a name yet?"

"Yes, I have gotten that far. His name is Kristopher Michael Long."

"Kris I love it! That is a beautiful way to honor Big Mike. I am so proud of you bringing it all together and making it work."

"Yea I am happy and less stressed. Mike is everything I prayed for and needed in a mate. Too bad I didn't figure that out before I got pregnant with another man's baby! I know and I know I am worth it.

Chapter 4

I have just been stuck on loser island that at times this is overwhelming to me. But in a good way. I am so in love with this man."

"Kris stop beating yourself up about that. You can't change that part. Terrance is out of the picture and you can move forward. Hey, now doesn't it feel good to be loved and in love like that?! I know the feeling cause big D and I mean that literally keeps me wanting more and coming back to get it. Mmmmm yeeeeees honey! All of him. Besides, everyone has had great sex with a loser. You're not the first and you won't be the last."

"Celeste girl bye! That is way more than I need to know about you! You are right though. Not many get it right on the first try."

"What? We are both grown, and it is apparent in your voice that you know exactly what time it is. When you get it and it's good girl-you want it more and as much of it as you can get."

"Well now big sis you do have a point. We made love once and oh my word Leesi-it was finger licking good! I have had some good wood but umm not like that. He took his time with me and made sure I was satisfied. AND that was withholding!"

"Dang girl, wait how do you know? If you said he went in like that what is he holding back on?"

"I know Mike. I have had a few of his past girlfriends talk about him to me. I even walked in on him and one girl some years back. With the way she was yelling one or two things were happening, she was dramatic as heck and she needed an award for her acting or he was putting in the work. He also warned me that he took it easy on me because of the baby and certain love making skills he wants to keep for his wife since his virginity is definitely off the table."

"Excuse me, huh what you say?! How do you feel about that?"

"I am fine with it. Somethings should be only explored in the safety and sanctity of the marriage bed. Your spouse shouldn't wonder if they were the only one or how many more you did that with before them. Now most people may not care or even think like that, but I do and ironically Mike does too. If you're not going to save yourself for marriage then by God at least save something! Too many times we give what should be husband perks to the boyfriends. Be cooking, cleaning, sexing, and washing their dirty draws trying to make them see you're the wife type. Then be somewhere mad when it doesn't work out knowing full well that all the signs were there, that they were Mr. Wrongs on all levels. But we lead with-we see his potential. Boo on us! A penis is not potential. What else can he offer? Now you married, and the husband has to unpack the baggage of the other men that hasn't been dealt with. But anyway, let me get off my soapbox! Besides, we will be married soon. Then we can give each other all we can stand of everything. There are some things I am holding out for him as well, so I respect how he feels about it."

"Girl you just told the truth about it all! Guilty to a degree! So wait, there are some sexual acts that you haven't done not even with Terrance?"

"Absolutely not! Girl definitely not! We were in an understanding. I knew that, so catching feelings was my fault. He is a ballplayer with all kinds of women falling all over him. I felt like he could have been out there doing whatever. He was getting his share of it all I am sure. The girl from the spa confirmed it, which was why I am so glad and felt no type of way because I didn't put my mouth on that or spend time trying to show him I was wifey material. Better believe every time we had sex, we used protection, and even that wasn't fool proof," she said rubbing her belly. "Again, I think that is something I should hold on to for my husband. Was Big D your first?"

"Technically, I tried it once with my first boyfriend and I didn't like it. I guess it is my wifely chore now. Kinda feel obligated because he is my husband, but he takes too long to get there, my jaws start hurting. In my mind, I be yelling hurry up joker and release-dang! Glad he doesn't feel the same way. That man is terrific at what he does in the bedroom. I guess that is the joys of a surgeon. He knows how to use his instruments. Speaking of, he just got out of the shower. The kids are asleep, I need to run my body across his and make him dirty again. Talk to you later sis!"

Blue sat for a second and looked at a phone that once had the voice of her sister on the other end. She wondered when she and Mike got married would she hurry and get off the phone to be with him. She had a hard time containing herself when she was around him as his new fiancé. She could only imagine what would happen when it is no restrictions or restraints, and he is her husband. She chuckled to herself. It blew her mind that she now saw her friend through the same eyes but in a different way. She saw him in a way that wanted to share and give all of herself to him. His loving her made her want to love him more. She regained focus and called her mom.

"Hey mommy!"

"Hey baby. How are you?"

"We are good. How are you guys?"

"We are making it. Big mama is not feeling too well, and I was making her some soup."

"Is she ok?"

She is fine. She just has a slight cold that's all. I am going to feed her this soup and a nice warm totty and put her in bed and then I am headed home. What's up?"

"We found out today we are having a boy. His name is Kristopher Michael Long."

"Oh Kristen. Are you guys excited?"

"Ma Mike is more excited than I am. We went to visit his parents and on the way back we stopped at the outlet and when I told Mike the baby was moving. We stood on the edge of the sidewalk I promise for 20 minutes and he just stooped down on his knee and started playing with the baby and the baby was responding. It was amazing to see. People were walking by awing us and congratulating us and taking pictures. I forgot to send you the video."

Just then her phone beeped. She hung up with her mom to take the call. It was Mike saying his mom saw the photo on the news titled *"Excited new dad."* He said it was big in their town and she had gotten multiple calls congratulating her on having a new grandchild and inquiring about the woman. It made a couple of good morning shows in the neighboring cities so it would probably be a matter of time before it headed to their area of town. Blue's mouth dropped. She wondered if since it was on the news had it hit any other social media platforms.

She grabbed her tablet started googling. There it was with almost a million views a short video of Mike kneeling and playing with little baby Long. The video was all over the internet, but it wasn't her video. Someone else recorded and posted it. She wasn't mad, just really surprised. As she searched, she gave Mike a play by play of what she saw and some of the comments. Strangers wishing them all the best on their new edition to their family. Blue was flabbergasted at the out pour of love they'd received from total strangers. She called her mother back and told her of their findings. She finished the conversation with her mother and laid and dosed off to sleep. She realized she had not called her closest friend.

"Hello darling," Blue greeted her friend.

"Hello godmother, how are you?"

Coco and Blue caught each other up on the what and what nots of their lives. She told her of the ended relationship with the football player and how he had begun to act a fool. She continued to tell her how he demolished her house due to their recent break up and her disdain for him due to the denial of their unborn child. Blue told her friend how she and Mike had finally succumbed to their feelings and planned to build their future together. She confessed that the situation with the baby was not ideal, but they loved each other and promised to work through it as they moved forward.

"Oh my God Kristen this is fantastic. I can't believe it. I am going to be an auntie. Kris oh I am so excited for you. They don't call that man the Black Stallion for nothing. Dang girl you got a good one. That is a real man. It is strenuous on a relationship when both parents have the baby together but you and Mike co-parenting with Terrance speaks volumes all the way around."

"No Coco there is no Terrance. He is adamant about this baby not being his so Mike and I are going to proceed right on along without him. We are having adoption papers drawn up and he will be signing the birth certificate."

"How is he denying this baby. Like on what grounds. Really? Well bye to him then. It is a blessing that Mike is willing to foot the responsibilities of dumb dumb's child. Girl you better always have that man's dinner on the table and some good loving waiting on him when he comes home!"

"That part! And uh, I got this Boo!" Blue promised.

"You better got this honey! Mike is one in a million. Men like him don't come often. How is his family taking all of the news? Do they know?" Coco asked cautiously.

"They know. Well his mom and dad know the baby is technically not his. They aren't holding it against me. They support us both, not just Mike. My mom and sister are the same way. Everybody is coming up to decorate the baby's room sometime soon. All the women will be painting and decorating while the men put together furniture and whatever else. Even Mike's parents may come. I hope they do. I am excited to have everyone under the same roof. You and Rod join us. It has been a minute since Mike and Rod have seen each other. I can cook a big meal or order pizza... yeah, I am going to order pizza for everyone. Heck, Mike may want to cook. He loves to."

"My Jesus, he cooks too? Girl, Rod don't know his way around the table let alone the stove. That's what's up. You got it good in your hood."

Blue and Coco continued on and on about the two men they were blessed to have in their lives. Coco reminded Blue that Rod's parents had to be put in check before they accepted her but whether they accepted her or not, Rod assured his family, she was well worth it. They were both glad they were complete within themselves and these men did not complete them, but simply enhanced and supported the women they were and were striving to be.

They rambled on about baby showers and baby gifts. They compared pregnancies and how their bodies had changed during this time in their lives. They both laughed at the way the men ogled over them and how the babies responded to their dads. They confessed their fears to each other out loud and cried as one consoled the other as they yearned to be good mothers as their moms were. Coco thanked Blue for allowing her to borrow her mom after her mother died. They expressed the advantages these babies would have that in some ways they were not afforded. By the time, the conversation was over, Blue found herself in a full out worship thanking God for his grace and his mercy even in this situation. Coco joined her friend and began to thank God for their future and their happiness.

"We can't let this much time pass between us again," Coco said between sniffles. "I need to go. Your brother-in-law is calling me as he is walking in the door. He left for the office a couple of hours early this morning to finish a major project. Here it is almost 11:30 at night and he is just getting home. When you own your own business, you put in the hours needed to prove yourself and make it work. He is getting ready to aggravate me and this child. We love you guys!"

"Well tell Rod I said hello. We love you too!"

They hung up and bedtime has called out to her. Mike called to check on her and made sure she set the house alarm. She let him know she complied with all his orders. She had given him a quick rundown of Monica and the baby. She put the phone to her stomach per Mike's request and allowed them to have some father son time. Mike talked and the baby would move anxiously to the sound of his voice. When she moved the phone, the baby settled back down. Blue silently thanked God that she didn't have to go through this alone. She had her best friend, and she was secured in her position as leading lady in his life. She felt sad and disappointed all in the same head space about the situation. She shrugged her shoulders and declared an "it was what is was" attitude and shook it off.

She made a vow not to cry anymore over things she couldn't control. She would no longer worry about the man who wouldn't, but the one who would. That was the last of the energy she would put toward Terrance and his lack of care or effort. She would continue to concentrate on the blessings she had been given and live in the moment of happiness of her future husband and child. By the time she had reached that decision she was awaken by her alarm clock. She heard Mike walk in the door. He left work a few minutes early assured to greet her and send her off for the day.

"Hey good morning. I was thinking, let's make the Christmas dinner a Christmas party. That way you can get all dressed up for me and we have an elegant dinner at the club instead of just jeans and t-shirt or khakis but really go all out."

"Ok that sounds great. What do you have up your sleeve Mr. Long?" she asked.

"Nothing Mrs. Long. I thought it would be nice to get the families and friends together for a good time at Big Mike's."

"Mmmmmmm Mike say it again!"

"Say it again!"

"Mrs. Long!" she giggled.

He began to sing it to her…. "Me and Mrs. Long we got a thiiiiiiing going ooonn."

He leaned down to kiss her and caught her forehead. Mike leaned down and greeted his son. The baby moved a little. They talked about his night and a few ideas he wanted to make happen at the lounge over the next several years.

"He is tired daddy. He moved most of the night. Now he wants to sleep."

"Hey, so what if the families stay over during the Christmas holiday? I know how much you love Christmas, and your biggest gift would be everyone we love right under the same roof."

"Okay babe. If you could make that happen, that would be great. That is perfect. I would love to see what our house would look like with both of our families in it."

"Yea me too. I am getting excited about the whole holiday thing. I am looking forward to it."

Blue showered and dressed for work. Her phone rang. Mike looked at the phone thinking it was her mom or sister at that time of the morning, but it was Big. He mumbled and reached for the phone. He decided not to answer it but the more he saw the number flashed across the face of her phone the angrier he became. He could not in his wildest imagination think why he would be so pressed or what could be so important that he would fix his fingers to dial her number. Blue walked into the room and locked eyes with Mike staring at her. He treaded very lightly not to accuse her of anything. However, he wanted to make sure there was nothing that would potentially put what they were building in jeopardy.

"Sooooo, do we need to change your number?"

"No. huh? Why? What are you talking about?" she asked hesitantly.

"While you were in the bathroom your phone rang. It was Terrance. Has he been calling or bothering you? Is there something I need to know?"

"Since you and I, this is the second time he has called me. I swear to you I have made it clear that we want nothing to do with him and to stop calling. I was not expecting him to call me again. It has always ended in a fight and we haven't had anything civil to say to each other since before the Georgia trip. Mike, I promise I will do whatever needed to keep him at bay. I love you and he is no threat to us. I would not be that stupid. I promise to God on all I have, I love you. Terrance is my past. I want you and this baby."

"I don't doubt it is over. I just know you can be nice. Not wanting to hurt feelings so I am just checking. Matter of fact, do I need to check him? You know I don't have any kind of a problem doing that? I won't have him stressing you and our child with dumb stuff. I will surely put that dude in his place about whatever he is calling you for. If he calls you again, I will be answering your phone."

Blue was taken aback for two reasons. For one, she had never been talked to like that by Mike and two it really turned her on that he had been assertive yet gentle all in the same tone as he put his foot down to her about Big. She felt her labia start to throb. She stood there and listened to him and replayed their first and only sexual encounter in her mind. She began to get even more bothered within her girl parts. He stood and looked at her in confusion. He wondered what was going on in her mind. She suddenly reached and kissed him. She felt his good stick press up against her. She jumped back and giggled. She had not expected to feel an erection. She liked it though. She liked it so much that she put her hand inside his pants and greeted his mini me good morning. He tried to play along as well. He was almost there when his phone rang.

"Dang! Darn! Damn it boy!" he picked up the phone. "What's going on Pops?"

"Nothing! Your mother and I just wanted to call you and let you know how proud we are of you son and the man you have become. I know it is early, did we interrupt anything?" he asked.

"If only you knew," he mumbled. "No sir you didn't. I was just getting home from the lounge and running Christmas plans by Kristen. Where is ma?" Mike asked.

"She is laying right here beside me. Well we didn't want anything except to tell you we love you and that you are a good man and son," he said.

"I love you guys too. Kiss mom for me and I will see you at Christmas. Will you and mom be ok to drive, or do I need to send a car for you?" Mike inquired.

"Son your mother and I will be fine. I know my way to you. I haven't gotten that old yet. Don't believe me get out of line and see can't I still give you that good old' left hook."

They laughed and ended the phone conversation. He focused his attention back to Blue. She stood in the doorway putting her shoes on.

"Where were we? Hey where are you going? Come here for a minute. I got somebody who wanted to meet you again." he said pulling her close.

"We were finished because I am going to be late for work. I love you but I am leaving. I wish we could pick this up where we left off when I get home from work. We gotta be strong bestie and fight it." she said patting his chest.

"Can't we break that? I know we promised to do this differently this time but whew. Lord help me to hold out!"

"As much as I want to let you inside me all night and most of the day we can't. We made a promise to God and each other. I am trying really hard not to disappoint Him anymore. We are going to have to wait until we get married. I know it sucks. I'm leaving. I love you."

"I love you too," he moped.

She left Mike standing in the floor. "We got to hurry and set a wedding date, or you and I are not going to make it." he said adjusting his little buddy. He went and took a showered and hoped it took the edge off, but he still had the thought of making love to his girl. He laid down and drifted off to sleep with her on his mind. On Blue's way to work Big called again. She sent him to voicemail. He called several times more before she answered.

"WHAT! WHAT! WHAT in the hell do you want with me? Why do you keep calling me? What is it that you want?"

"Dang girl why you on 100 this morning? I was calling to let you know I am in town and I was hoping to come through and see you. I know things between us have not been good lately. I miss you girl and I need to see you. I didn't think I could just use my key and come in since I hadn't seen you in a while. I figured I might get caught with a bat again."

"No sweetheart this time you will catch a bullet. I don't live there anymore. I have told you there is nothing you can say to me to let you back in our lives. You surely cannot get back in my bed and certainly not between my legs with the temper tantrums you threw. That part of us is over and I have moved on and I am not going to tell you again not to call me. Don't make me change my number."

"My bad. So you are having my baby?"

"Uuuuuuummmm no sir, the little bastard is not yours. Isn't that what you said? I am having Mike's baby. You gave up those rights and I will not keep letting you make me feel bad for something you helped me do. We may have screwed and got him, but I guarantee you won't have to worry about helping me raise him."

"Oh so it is a boy? "You saying I got a son? Hoe you would have a boy."

"No no no no sir, I have a son. You wanted no part of this remember. You have whatever life it is you have. So please go back to doing whatever it is you do. You can hide up under a rock for all I care just don't call me again. You have your life and I have a new life to think about. I have moved clear past on. Please let me go," Blue pleaded.

"Trick since you say we have a son together; I am not letting go of nothing until I see you. I need to see you. I don't care about the baby. Why can't it go back to the way it used to be? But no, you thought it was just going to be over-you were just going to get away from me that easily Blue, huh? Oh I have friends that will follow you and kill you if I just say the word, but I wanna take joy and pleasure in making you miserable between football seasons. You left me-just like the rest of them and now you gonna have to pay for your sins and theirs. If I can't have you nobody can especially not that punk," he roared. "Tell me Blue, could you go on with your life if you were dead?" he laughed.

"Why? How did we get to this place?" her voice trembled. "Terrance listen to yourself. Are you threatening to kill me?"

"No that is a promise. You won't be able to get away from me. I will find out where you live. There is no running from me Kris, you can't shake me baby. I am not worried about jail. I am at the height of my career. Nobody will believe anything you say about this situation. You will look like the crazy groupie. I plan on making your life miserable for the next 18 years, if I don't kill you first, so watch your back."

"Terrance please hear me when I say you may not be afraid of jail, but I will surely send your soul to hell. I will kill you if you come anywhere near my family. Honey, you haven't experienced my crazy. Please Terrance let it go. Let me go. Let us go. I need you not to call me or come anywhere near us!"

Blue hung up the phone. Distraught, she pulled over on the side of the road. Her nerves overtook her. She began to sweat and breathe uncontrollably. She called her sister and tried to tell her what happened, but few words formed. Through her tears, she gasped for air. Big called back again. He continued to call back-to-back leaving voicemail after voicemail and text after text. Consumed by the stress of it all, she felt her body began to shut down. She considered herself to be resilient, but this took her out of her element. It never occurred to her the depths he would try and go to make her life miserable for sport. She never suspected his evil ran so deep. She didn't know this new guy and it scared her to the core. This was way out of pocket even for him. The more she thought, the more her thoughts and the situation overshadowed her. Sharp pains ripped through her stomach leaving it in knots. Pain hurled through her body locking and constricting her movement. She heard Celeste but she responded with no words, she was reduced to moans and whimpers that vaguely carried over the phone.

Celeste hung up and called Mike and told him what happened. Mike quickly dialed 911 and gave the dispatch operator a description of the jeep and her potential location since he knew her route to work and how long it took to get there from the house. Mike grabbed his shoes and a sweatshirt and frantically drove her same route to work praying to find her. Mike arrived first, he fled his car and ran to her side. He pleaded with her to hold on. Shortly, local authorities and EMS arrived. She was flushed and drenched with sweat. Pushing him out of the way, the EMS workers put her on a stretcher and immediately gave her oxygen. She opened her eyes and reached for Mike right before she passed out. He tried to get to her but was blocked.

Mike followed the ambulance to the hospital and called his homeboys to pick up Blue's jeep. He called Celeste back and gave her an update on her sister. She called their mom and they made provisions to be with Blue within hours. Mike called Ms. Deb and told her what happened. Mike thought before he and Blue could get started good, it had the deadly potential to be over. He described the state of his best friend and love to his dad and began to break down. He loved Blue with all he had for a long time. The thought of it falling apart and slipping away was more than he wanted to face. He tried to stay positive, but he could only think about life with his best friend no longer in it. Mike not only worried about the condition she was in, but he was also concerned with the baby. His eyes were filled, and his heart was heavy. He slowly began to grieve the *"what ifs"* of what had happened with the woman and child he loved. He began to replay the brief conversation between he and Celeste.

He wondered what happened so bad that it sent Blue to the hospital. He looked down at her phone and saw all of the missed calls and unanswered text from Big. Mike was enraged with anger and fury as he skimmed the text. A fighter Mike was not however, he knew how to throw hands if need be. He felt it was his duty to find Terrance and reward him with a special ass whooping for the hell that landed her on the side of the road unconscious. He deemed it his right as the man in her life to set some proper boundaries.

He needed to send a clear message for him to stay the hell away from his family. He prayed for eight years for the time to come when he would spend every day with her. He was not about to let some looser blow that for him. When they arrived at the hospital the first face Mike saw was Mr. Jim's. He was headed back home from taking the kids to school when Ms. Deb called him and told him what happened to Blue.

Mike and Mr. Jim embraced. Mr. Jim assured Mike that Blue was a fighter, and she would be fine. They walked in the emergency room together. The doctors guaranteed Mike they would do all they could for her and the best thing for him to do was to sit and wait. Mr. Jim talked him through some of his anger and hurt. He made certain to Mike that the best thing he could do for Kristen was to be in prayer for her.

Mike wiped his tears and began begging God for Kristen's life. He prayed that God would heal and restore because he loved her, and he couldn't live without her.

An hour later the doctor came out to greet him. He assured Mike as they ran test and ruled out speculation he would let him know. As family arrived Mike shared with them what was shared with him. A few more hours passed. The doctor came out and spoke to the family about Kristen's condition.

"Family I know this is a difficult time and you all want answers. We ran multiple test and bloodwork, and they all came back inconclusive. We can only conclude that Ms. Stancil had a severe panic attack that mimicked a stroke possibly even a heart attack. It caused her body major stress and triggered her blood pressure to spike which was why she passed out. Thankfully, we were able to stabilize her. We also gave her a round of fluids. She and the baby are looking to make a full recovery. He has a strong will like his mother. We gave her a sedative, so she is sleeping for right now. I can permit you all to rotate in the room to see her. You must hold it together and not put any more stress on her than she is already under. We will keep Ms. Stancil under close watch for the next seventy-two hours just to make sure she is progressing as needed and there are no additional findings. You all may go in two at a time but again don't allow her to talk just comfort and encourage her to rest."

Mike and Mama Bella visited first. Mike decided that everyone would be visiting one at a time because he was not leaving her side. Although there was nothing he could do for her but pray he wanted to do it next to her. He held her hand and whispered in her ear gently touching her face making his presence known. He leaned in and kissed her belly as their son slowly responded. Any business that needed handling he did with a click of his phone. His business partner checked in and kept him abreast of the contracts in the new space. He hadn't told

Blue all the details of the place. He wanted to surprise her. He kissed her and whispered, "I love you" in her ear. She mustered up enough strength to squeeze his hand and shed a slight stream of tears.

Chapter 5

Evening came and found them all still sitting around watching and waiting. They finally persuaded Mike to step out and at least get something to eat. He had been awake since the night before she fell into this unfortunate mishap. Their mothers assured him that she would be fine until he got back, and Kristen needed him to do what he needed to do to keep himself from falling apart. She knew it didn't mean he loved her any less. It just meant that he needed to be ok as well. Heading home to change clothes Mike grabbed a bite to eat. His mind began to wonder. He wondered where the low life Terrance was and what he would do to him if he saw him.

No sooner than he had that thought Mike pulled into the gas station. He saw a man who looked like the one he was looking for. As he got closer he realized that was him. On the passenger side was some female. He stood there smiling with no care in the world and no inkling of Blue's condition. Mike became infuriated as he watched while the man who put his love in the hospital was out having the time of his life while Blue fought for hers. Mike parked the car and jumped out. Just as Big reached to open the door to get in his car, he is pulled back and punched in the nose. Mike hit him in the mouth and again in the mouth two more times.

He grabbed him and threw him to the ground. He straddled him and continued to use his face as a punching bag. Mike beat him until his soul was partially satisfied. He could have beat him some more, but he wanted to get home, showered and back to his love. The female screamed as she spectated her Boo catching a beat down.

"If you ever come near her again I swear I will kill you. Stay away from Blue and our son. You got that? Stay the hell away from her," he said kicking him one last time.

Mike turned and walked away giving Big no time to get up or respond. He got back in his jeep and drove off. The onlookers stood by, scratched their heads, and talked amongst themselves after they watched that piece of the puzzle unfold. One guy tried to video but was only able to record the last part of it. He felt a little better sending that message. At this point in the game it could be hit or miss. Mike didn't know if Big would retaliate and come after him or try and take it out on Blue again. He felt justified in making it known man to man that they were not just going to allow him to be reeking all types of havoc and they just took it. He needed to be clearly understood that she and Mike were a united front. His phone rang. It was his homeboy Eric.

"Yo man, you good? How is baby girl? What is the doctor saying?"

"What's up man? She is still sedated to help her get some rest. She had a severe panic attack that mimicked a stroke. She is a fighter, so we are praying for a speedy recovery and for her to come home soon. The medication hasn't worn off, so she doesn't have the strength to open her eyes yet. While she is resting I ran out to shower and grab something to eat."

"Well son if there is anything I can do let me know aight."

"Thanks E. I appreciate that man. My phone is beeping let me get this. It's her sister." he clicks over. "Hey Celeste. Is Kris ok?" he asked.

"Yea she is fine. Still sleeping. I just wanted to check on you. Hey, is it okay that since we are all here we get some stuff together for the baby's room? Just to take the edge off and give us all something to look forward to."

"Yeah sure. That would be great. I am sure she would love to see that when she comes home. I am almost home. I will be back in about thirty minutes. When she wakes up I have to be there."

"Ok well she is doing better. She is still sleep but she is moving more. The doctor is allowing us to all stay in the room with her now. Hurry up and get back because you know you are going to be the first one she calls for. She loves you dude."

"I love her too Celeste."

"Oh don't I know it. It was very sweet of your parents to come and be with us. We greatly appreciate it Mike. My sister is marrying into a great family. She is really blessed."

"Thanks sis, but I feel like I am the blessed one. It is going to be interesting to see how we all function under the same roof."

"Yea! It will be great! See you in a few."

They hung up. He pulled up to the house and was greeted by the men and kids. In haste Mike warned Delmar about what Celeste wanted to do and he was about to be an accomplice. Delmar's phone rang. Celeste called to tell him the plans she had for fixing up the baby's room. Delmar took his marching orders. He implored help from Mr. Long, and he agreed, and they left the house taking the children to Ms. Deb's so Jenna could watch them. Mike ran in the bathroom, took a quick shower, and threw on a t-shirt and sweats. On the way back out the door he saw her ring on her dresser. He grabbed it and his coat and closed the door behind him. Mr. Long was happy to oblige with helping however he could for his first grandchild. The men got busy putting together the furniture and doing whatever else was instructed.

Once Mike got back to the hospital the ladies left to go shopping for the bedding and decorations for little Kristopher's room. They met the men at the store to get the paint. While Mike stayed with Blue the family worked at putting the baby's room together. They spent the night putting together furniture, painting, and hanging pictures. "The window in the room lets in the perfect amount of sunlight." Mrs. Long noted. "They can care for him in his room and take advantage of the beautiful view." Mama Bella said through her tears.

She was so grateful that the situation wasn't as bad as it seemed. Celeste comforted her mother. She assured her that Blue was ok. They found space where they could and slept until morning. Giving them time to get up and stir around, Mike called to let the family know Blue was awake and asking for everyone. It was too late to call them last night, so he promised to call everyone first thing the next morning. The family lifted praises and thanks to God. They needed that news.

It was a sign of the good things they knew were to come. The family hurried down the highway to the hospital. They came in the room and gathered around her. The doctors were in agreeance that she could go home as scheduled within the next forty-eight hours or sooner. There were tears of joy from everyone. She sat up in confusion. She did not fully remember what happened to her and how she winded up in the hospital. Celeste began to explain to her what happened. Mike stepped in and finished the rest of the incident. Blue became frantic. Her mother pleaded with her get herself together and calm down before something happened again. It took her a few minutes, but she settled back down. She could not believe she let him get to her this bad. Celeste helped Blue take a shower and put on some of her own clothes. Mike helped her get on the bed and then sat down beside her.

"Bae?" Mike whispered.

"Yes Love?" she replied.

"You scared out hell out of me-out of us. I pray to God we never have to experience anything like that again." he said.

"Mike baby," she interrupted.

"No Blue let me finish. I am so in love with you. I thought I was going lose to you and I could not stand even the thought of that let alone that being the reality. I have loved you for the past eight years and I know I said we could do this when you were ready but after seeing you in this situation, it has made me want to speed up the process and officially begin our forever together. Loving you is right, and it just makes sense to make this official. I plan to be with you all the time I have in this lifetime. I gave you this ring and told you to try it out but now I don't want you to just try it. You even said you want to be married before our son is born. We have about four months to do that, so I want us to be real about this. Blue in front of God and our families baby please say yes and marry me?"

"Yes officially Mike I will! I love you too baby. I thank God that He put you in my life even eight years ago. I am more than honored to marry you my best friend!" she said through tears.

The families began to cheer and bid them congratulations. In all the excitement Mike reached into his pocket and pulled out her ring. Everybody's eyes fixed in on the ring. The night was turning into one they could remember.

"Dang son you didn't tell your old man you were holding. Let me borrow twenty dollars. My boy I knew you would handle your business," said his dad proudly.

They all smiled and cooed over the ring. It was official, the dream was well on its way to becoming a reality. It was not just talk but it was now endorsed. He had given her the ring earlier, but she didn't really wear it. They had not really started making plans. The ring on the finger solidifies their love and them being serious enough to set the plan in motion. During the celebration, the police knock on her hospital room door.

"Sorry to trouble you folks but we are looking for Michael Long. We were told he could be found here," they said.

"I am Mike Long what seems to be the problem officers?" he asked.

"The problem is sir; we have a warrant for your arrest for assault on one Terrance Belton. Can you tell us what happened?" they asked trying to keep the situation at a minimum.

"Are you serious? That punk son of a....." he paused and took a deep breath. "He called my fiancée two days ago and caused her such stress that she went into a panic attack that mimicked a stroke. Which was why I could be found here! The pretty lady in the bed is my future wife," he said getting agitated. He pulled out her phone and showed the officers the text messages and all of the missed calls. Some were even as current as that day.

"Woow is that true ma'am?" they asked.

"Yes!" everyone agreed unanimously.

"What was the nature of all this?" the police inquired.

"We used to date, and I broke it off almost six months ago and he called me out of nowhere making threats to me and my unborn child. He told me he would kill me. I got so upset I had to be hauled off in an ambulance from the side of the road," she explained.

"Yea, hey, I thought you looked familiar. I ran that call ma'am; I was there yesterday. I didn't think you were going to make it. It was pretty bad. I am sorry that happened to you. I tell you what. I know Terrance Belton is a big shot football player but to do that to a lady. Do me a favor try to avoid him, and we will pretend this never happened. We will document all of the calls and text messages as well. What man takes another man downtown for assault? Never did really like the guy. Look here, enjoy the rest of your night with your family and ma'am we sure are glad you pulled through. The nerve of that guy. You ladies and gentlemen have a good night."

The officers tilted their hats and left. The families thanked them and assured them that there would be no more problems from them on their end.

"Michael what in the world did you do?" his mom asked.

"I saw him at a gas station yesterday and before he could get in his car I just hand a little hand to face conversation with him while telling him to stay away from my family!" he shrugged.

"See son this is exactly what I was worried about. What if he tries to hurt you? Oh Lord!" shouted his mother.

"Ma calm down I got this. He is just being stupid right now it will all blow over soon. Trust me. I am sure pops would do the same for you." he said with assurance.

"Sure I did," Mr. Long smirked.

"When Eddie?" she asked.

"Remember in '66 Johnny *no thumbs* White?" he asked her.

"Yea. What about him?" she asked.

"He used to like you and picked on you every day, right?"

"We were kids. What are you talking about?" she asked.

"One day I caught him in the bathroom and beat the brakes off him for bothering you and to show him I meant business I took his milk money for a week. You noticed how he just left you alone. A good butt whoopin' don't matter when you're doing it for the one you love!" he grinned.

"Eddie!" she gasped.

"Look, as her mother. This is no picnic in the park for me either," Ms. Bella chimed in.

"Ma, you don't have to worry about me. I chose to be with her, and she is not causing the drama. He is. Mama Bella my job is to protect her and that is what I will do. As for you Kristen Stancil. I love you and I will never stop loving you. I am looking out for you and I really don't care what anybody has to say," he assured them.

"Michael are you referring to me? You are my son," she whimpered.

"Not just you. Anybody. With all due respect I am a grown man, and I knew Blue was pregnant with another man's baby when we ventured into this. Trust me we are good. I love you Ma," he says.

"But Michael!" she yelled.

"Baby let it alone now, our son is a grown man. We should trust that he knows what he is doing. It will all work out darling," he said trying to calm her down.

"I love Mike and I did not pick this situation. As a matter of fact, we found out I was pregnant while discussing our feelings for each other. By then we were liking the idea of being in love and it was too late. I would never do anything to hurt Mike Mama Long and I need you to know that I love him." she said.

"Kristen I am sorry. Seeing my son almost get picked up by the police was something I had never experienced before. I know you would never put my son in harm's way. But still." she apologized.

"Thank you mama Long," she said.

They hug and show no ill will or hard feelings toward each other. After that awkward moment Celeste mentions the baby's room to break the ice. They begin to laugh and talk again.

"Soooooo what happened while I was out," Blue asked.

"Well we all got together and went ahead and decorated the baby's room. Kris you are going to love it," the ladies spoke up.

"Oooooh really guys? I bet it is beautiful! Did you guys bring pictures?" Blue asked. "Well I definitely did my part by staying out of the way."

"Uuuum no we wanted to surprise you, and yeah you did. This was not how we expected you to follow directions," Celeste said.

"Well I would have been surprised with pictures Celeste," Blue whined.

"No Boo. You need to rest up the last day so you can blow this joint. We need to celebrate this baby and his life. Let's not forget this new engagement!" Celeste cheered.

"I know Leesi. Oh my God I know my patients are like what the world," she said.

No sooner than she said that her staff walked through the door. They held her office down. Ms. Deb kept them abreast with her situation. They came in with balloons and cards. The greeted her with well wishes. As they talked and laughed the doctor came in. He was making his rounds to check on Blue and the baby. She assured the family that Blue was recovering at great speed and that she could be released to go home the next morning. Everyone had a sigh of relief. Thanking God that the worst was over, and she could go on with her life. It would still be a few days before she could go back to work. Her staff promised that they would continue to hold the fort down until she returned. She gave them explicit instructions on what else needed to be done and thanked them over and over for their loyalty to her and the children and families they served.

She especially wanted to thank Mr. Tomas for being a God send and being able to care for her patients as well as her. The room was filled with voices of love and laughter. She was feeling better so her family and friends decided it was ok to go home. Blue held tight to her niece and nephew. Little Delmar reached down and put his hand on her stomach and spoke, "Baby." She kissed him and they left. The parents all went out together after saying their goodnights. Since it was still a little early they all went back to Mike's house to straighten up and to shift some things around so Mike and Blue would not have it to worry about it when he brought her home the next morning.

Jenna climbed in the bed beside Blue and whispered in her ear. "I am glad you are feeling better and I am glad God healed you. I love you and don't know what I would do without you. You are my other mom and big sister and best friend all in one." Blue began to shed tears and grabbed Jenna hugging her as tight as she could. Blue also comforted her by letting her know the feeling was indeed mutual. Mr. Jim and Ms. Deb informed Blue they would see her over the weekend. Finally the room cleared. There was no one there but her and Mike.

"I want to apologize again for my mom baby," Mike began.

"Why Mike? She was right," Blue insisted.

"No Kris, she wasn't and even if she was in front of everyone was not the time to voice it. I know she is my mom. However, I am a grown man and I love you. This is my life and my choices to make," he said.

"Mike, baby I understand where she is coming from. It is ok. I honestly thought I could handle him this time like I did the last time he called." she said.

"Hold up, what do you mean he called the last time?" Mike asked.

"Well he called once before. I told you that in the house the other day. I made it clear on my end that I didn't want him or want anything from him. Mike I swear to you that I am not stringing you along and I am not playing any games. I just thought I could handle it myself. I didn't want to drag you in this mess but look at us now. I know babe I just thought I could handle it," she said.

"Wait wait Blue I know you would never do anything to hurt me. I am sorry I didn't mean to make it seem like I doubted you. I know you would never do anything to jeopardize us. And baby you are supposed to tell me if someone is threatening you. My job is to protect you and

I will do that," he promised. "So are we changing your number?!" he asked.

"Yea, we can go ahead and call them now," she agreed.

Mike crawled on the bed and held her. She put her hand in his and admired his love for her on her left ring finger. He put his hand on her belly and stirred up the baby. As Mike moved his hand across Blue's belly the baby seemed to move with him. The nurse walked in the room and told them the doctor ordered another ultrasound on the baby. They rolled her down to the examining room and proceeded with the examination of the baby. It took a moment to find it but suddenly they heard a strong steady heartbeat. Then on the monitor they saw him. Blue and Mike felt gratitude in their hearts that came with knowing baby Long was ok. He too had pulled through. He kissed his lover while they waited to be taken back to their room. The doctor made check out official for them bright and early the next morning.

The sooner she got out the sooner she could get back to her life and put this week behind her. She called the phone company and changed her number. Now the only way Big could get to her would be through the office. It would be hard unless he waited outside. She doesn't answer phones and he would not be allowed to just walk through the doors that led to where she saw her precious patients. Blue desperately wanted morning to come. She was dying to see the room that everyone lovingly spent so much time on. Besides the little hospital incident, her life was coming along better than she could have ever imagined. Even though it may not have been special to anyone else she knew it was a beautiful thing for someone to love and care for her in a way that she had never known but quickly got used to. She in turn loved him from a place within herself she didn't realized existed.

She thought she had maxed out her love and was simply going through the motions and forcing it with Big. Once he was out of the picture and she gave way to the idea of Mike, she opened her heart and mind to him and everyday had been great between them. Then she remembered Mike was the prayer she prayed in her prayer closet. The prayer she'd asked God for-to send her Boaz, the one that was designed just for her. God was faithful and did so. It was an indescribable feeling knowing that God answered her prayer. Their love began to shape their journey on the path to becoming one. It radiated to all those around them. Mike climbed back in the bed with her and held her tight. Over in the night, they were disturbed by the nurse coming in to take the last round of vitals before Blue could finally be released.

Morning came with a song of freedom. She was ready to go home. While she waited for the nurse to wheel her out she begged and pleaded with Mike to take her to breakfast. He wanted to get her home and rested. He declined her sweet plea and agreed to prepare the whole family breakfast. He persuaded her to sit and enjoy this beautiful Autumn Thursday with her loved ones. She agreed and he was able to stick to his guns until he looked at her beautiful face and decided he needed to spend just one more hour alone with her even if it was over pancakes and eggs in a restaurant. Blue was discharged and they hurried off to a cozy breakfast place. They requested the booth way in the back isolated from the other tables and there they sat for the next two hours talking about their future. They basked in the joy of being engaged and talked intently about wedding plans. They finished their meal, and he took her home. They walked in to be greeted by their families.

The house was full of early morning love and laughter. The kids were up and playing, the ladies were talking and laughing. Gospel music played at low volume on the radio. Mike and Blue loved the feel of their home. Mike sat with Blue under a blanket while Delmar and Mr. Long made breakfast for the women and children. They sat in the living room and continued to talk and laugh as they waited on breakfast. The fragrance of bacon and sausage filled the air as the aromas of pancakes, home fried potatoes and eggs dressed in sharp cheese danced within their nostrils. The sweet finish of the maple syrup had the house smelling like a small country diner. Mr. Long surprised the house with his famous grits.

The table was set, and it was time to eat. Mike and Blue stayed on the couch. They cuddled, laughed, and talked with the family as they ate. Blue laid her head on Mike and dozed off and on waiting for everyone to finish breakfast. Mike suggested Blue go and lay down, but she wanted the best of both worlds. The joy and comfort of laying in her companion's arms and watching her two families enjoy the company of each other. She was at peace right there on the couch basking in her life and all the beauty within it. She felt the baby becoming restless and kicking. The pain grew a bit uncomfortable. She nudged Mike and told him the issue she was having, and Mike began to rub her stomach and Baby Long calmed down a bit.

"Babe you good?" he asked.

"Yeah. I promise I thought I was about to go into labor. That got really serious really quick!" she said.

"What is he doing now?" he asked. "You probably got gas. Don't you fart beside me! Don't make me love you different!" he jokes.

"Really dude?" she sarcastically chuckled. "Right now thanks to you he is calm. But gas though. Love me, love my farts. Simple," she shrugged. "Like for real, I don't know what it was, but he needs to get it together."

"Leave my lil man alone. He's alright. He hears his family all in the same room and he's trying to come out and meet them. He wants to chill with his uncle D and his daddy!"

"Well, if he continues to feel like he is in here kicking, swimming and horseback riding, I am going to let you carry him for the duration of his incubation and see if you like that. My womb is not big enough for his little butt to be in there turning flips!"

Mama Bella saw Blue's discomfort and reassured her that it was probably gas. She cut her eyes sharply at Mike to find him laughing in agreement with her mom. Blue told them how the baby and Mike had a great relationship already and how the baby responds to him. The ladies assured her she would find that to be a good thing during those late-night feedings. The men agreed that mid-night feedings were the worst, and they were glad when the kids started sleeping through the night. They shared their different experiences of parenting giving the new couple encouragement promising them they were going to need it.

Changing the subject, they reminded Blue and Mike about the baby's room. They hurried her slowly to the room. Celeste opened the door leaving Blue and Mike stunned with what they saw. They embraced each other and Blue laid her head in Mike's chest and began to cry. The blue and white baseball themed room was more than they imagined. There was a gray colored crib complete with matching dresser and changing table. On the corner of the dresser sat a baseball lamp. His crib had baseball bedding with the crib bumper and pillows off to the side. On the painted blue walls was a shelf.

On it sat a baseball bat with his name on it. Beside the bat was an autographed baseball. Mounted in a picture frame was Mike's old college baseball jersey. On his ceiling a picture of a baseball field. On the floor was a large plush carpet in the color and shape of a baseball. There was a baseball bat rug at the doorway entry. Off in the corner close to the doubled pane window was a beautiful, oversized rocking chair decorated to match the room and carved in the chair was his last name that Mr. Long had carved himself. The view outside his window overlooked a beautiful lake out back. She envisioned them sitting in his room feeding him. She smiled as she played clips in her mind of the late-night feedings and diaper changes. Seeing his room made her want to have him there in her arms immediately. They stood in anticipation for the awaited arrival of baby Long. In everybody's mind Mike and Blue were proud parents of a baby boy.

It didn't matter to them that Mike was not the biological father. They celebrated the loved that was shared in the life being carried in Blue's womb. Blue and Mike continuously thanked their families for the rest of the evening. The women sat around and talk and watched the children play. The men played a long run of Spades then went out back for beers and a few games of horseshoes. They ordered pizza for dinner. It was the perfect and better than Blue imagined. Morning came and everyone went back to their separate living habitats. It was Friday night and Mike went off to the lounge leaving Blue to rest. He didn't want to leave her, but business called, and he had to answer.

It was the busiest weekend of the lounge and everything had to be perfect. Blue didn't see much of Mike. Much of his time was at the lounge or asleep. Sunday Mike slept in and Kristen went to church. After church Kristin took Jenna to the mall and out to lunch. They sat and talked for hours about school, boys, music, and even potential colleges. It was much needed and well spent time together. Kristen dropped Jenna off and went home to prepare herself for the work week. The week moved rather swiftly. Friday finally arrived and it was to be spent with Blue's family. Mama Bella was preparing her pre-Thanksgiving dinner. She cooked a small feast for them. It was a typical Thanksgiving meal with turkey, dressing, green bean, casseroles, cranberry sauce, collards, cabbage, macaroni and cheese, corn, potato salad and cornbread. To wash it all down was a choice of her mom's special Thanksgiving punch. They sat, laughed, ate, napped, and ate some more. Then Blue's mom packed them a few plates to go. On the way home Blue slept.

Blue and Mike returned home. He gently shook her to wake her up. He pulled in the garage and reminded her that they would be in hiding for the rest of the weekend. No interruptions. Thanksgiving was fast approaching, so he wanted a quiet relaxing few day at home with just the two of them. He'd made a small fortune off of the events he'd done last weekend which turned into yearly contractual accounts. He was spotlighted in the local magazine and newspaper again for the way and his staff executed those events. Mike's Lounge ranked number one in the city and rising steadily at number one across the state.

Chapter 6

His phone rung seemingly off the hook with potential clientele. He figured it was time to hire a personal assistant to help take the load off of him so he could really focus on his family. He gave his staff an additional bonus and this well-deserved weekend off. His staff was the backbone of his establishment and he always showed his appreciation for them. They got out of the car and he carried their bags in the house. He locked the door and they tucked themselves away. They took one more look in the baby's room and then moved into Mike's room to cuddle on the bed and watch television. It was almost one o'clock in the morning when they realized they had leftovers.

Blue warmed up a plate for the two of them to share. Leftovers seemed to taste better at that time of morning. Before long they were full and sleep. Alarms sounded. They pushed the off buttons and continued to sleep tucked into one another. They both needed the rest, so they took full advantage of it. They woke to mid-morning small talk. They reminisced about college and what life could have possibly been like if they would have dated when they first met. They were thankful for the time they had been best friends, but they were also grateful for the now. The now that started their happily ever after. Mike got up and fixed them a late lunch/early dinner. The smell from the kitchen was delightful. Waiting for lunch made her hangry. She was always ready to eat. Blue walked towards the kitchen tripped over nothing, and almost fell. Mike ran and caught her before she hit the floor.

"Babe oh my God! You can't keep it together lately." he said.

"Ha! I guess not. If my balance is off now, imagine when I get in my last trimester. My sugar might be low. You are taking forever to feed us. You know eating is my favorite pastime lately. I will grab an apple while I wait on you to finish. I do love falling into your arms though."

He kissed her. In between kisses he assured her that drastic measures would never have to be a reason to fall in his arms. Mike let her know that his arms awaited her any time she needed them. He made it very clear that he loved and supported her and as best he could, he would always be there for her. She believed him. She would like to seal the moment with some much-needed love making. Between her recent visit to the hospital and the little boy in her womb showing out, she craved his love making to put out the fire she housed for him.

On top of it all, her heart fluttered every time he spoke, touched, or kissed her, any thought of him made her body thirst him. She desired Mike the way she desired no other man. To open herself to her mate completely was something she had been dying to do for years. Now to be in that space was satisfying! She was ready to set the wedding date and really show her love for him. She knew the first time he took it easy on her. She understood his love making ability was a force to be reckoned with and she needed to be a hundred percent when it came to riding that stallion.

Her body, mind, and soul aligned with her heart to love him, to want to make love to him and only him until death did them part. She followed him around in the kitchen. She got close to him and breathed him in. Being with him made it hard for her to remember what it was like in the past with anyone else. The way he loved her made all the others irrelevant. He had a genuine want and desire for her and she for him. She was fully aware of the gentle yet strong God-fearing man she had in front of her. He finished cooking and Blue was in her happy place. Mike wasn't God but his love for her sure was heavenly.

"That meal was amazing. Do you cook like that often?" she joked.

"Nope, just when I am trying to impress a potential lady friend. How am I doing?"

"Not bad sir. Not bad at all. The doctor made me a follow up appointment with my primary doctor for her to check the baby again. That will be on my things to do list this week."

"Ok what time. Oh, I meant to tell you the parties were a huge success last weekend. I checked the website and we got rave reviews. My staff really had my back with making sure everything was in place and ready to go. They followed my instructions to the letter. They even gave a special shout out to my lead bartender. She helped me organize much of it. She wants to own her own business, so I pushed her to venture out and learn a thing or two. She was mad but look at the success of it.

"Oh my that is fantastic! I knew once you hired the right staff that team would be phenomenal. Baby you don't have to go. It is not a big deal. I should be in and out."

"You are right. I don't have to go but I am. What time is the appointment?"

"I don't know. I have to wait for the office to call me and give me the time."

They continued to talk and laugh. They rambled on about the other relationships from previous years and how they were both equally surprised at whom the other chose to date. They even laughed and mocked each other's choice of mate. They hadn't laughed like this in a while and they remembered something very important. They remembered that even with everything going on they were not just friends. They were best friends, and they must never lose sight of that. They remembered how to keep it light. They remembered to let loose and clown each other as they always had. It had been a few stressful months and to sit and laugh together was needed between the couple. Mike reminded Blue on her way to the kitchen to pick her feet up and be careful not to let the floor grab her foot and make her fall.

She stuck her tongue out at him but thought about what he said. She helped him clean the kitchen. They laughed and spent time enjoying each other. They went back to the living room. The radio was on. He keenly tuned into the low sounds coming from it. His eyes got big. He grabbed the remote and turned it up. It was one of his favorite love songs. He helped Blue off the couch and asked her to dance with him in the middle of their floor. They hold each other as close as they can and sway from side to side. The dance turned into dancing as they enjoyed the next few songs that played. They left the floor when the DJ played the wrong song. Mike cut the radio back down and they agreed to a movie. It was still a little early, but late enough for them to want to crawl back on the bed and watch a little television. She followed Mike in his room and snuggled under the covers and channel surfed. They watched television and he gently stroked her arm and shoulder. She occasionally ran her hand across his leg and chest.

"I respect the fact that we want to wait to make love, but I promise I am intoxicated with you and I want to physically get more acquainted with your inner anatomy. I just feel the urge to lay inside you. Uuuuugh! Do you really know how much I love you lady?"

"Yes sir I do. This has not been easy for me either. I want to make love to you as the song said- all night long. To be molded into your body and allow our souls to touch. When you walk past me I want to rip your clothes off with my teeth and just kiss and suck on each part of your body."

They both bust out in laughter to the point of tears. They tried to get serious but each time they looked at each other it was impossible to keep a straight face. He looked at her and confessed that he wanted to kiss her with it leading to other things, but since they took a vow of celibacy he went into the kitchen and came back with a glass of ice water. She laughed at him only to realize he was serious.

"You can still kiss on me Mike."

"No Blue I can't. Kissing will lead to something else and I am trying to respect the fact we want to remain abstinent until we get married. Besides, I don't feel at ease making love to you and lil man is literally in between us. I will but I won't like it a whole lot. You don't understand the magnitude in which I am dying to make love to you. I took it easy on you the first time. I am ready to get in there, handle my business and make your eyes cross and your body quiver."

"Well, since we can't do that," she blushed, "let's talk about our wedding day. We love each other and we know we are making plans to get married before little baby Kris gets here. Are we ready to set a date? I didn't know if you already had something in mind."

"Well I wanted to surprise you. I already have what I would love to do in honoring you as my bride. Will you trust me enough to execute my plan and yes as a matter of fact you can have your dress by the middle of December. That is all you need to know and that my dear is too much."

"Well dang babe. How can I help? I trust you but do you think you can handle it?"

"Yes ma'am. I told you I got you. I don't want you to have to lift a finger or worry about anything until after baby boy is born. You have plenty of time to be stressed out after he gets here. Babe please let me do this, and yes I can handle it. I have been waiting on this moment since the day I laid eyes on you. I got this. Trust me!"

"I do and I will. You sound like you have it all together. I was just asking. This too is new to me. I am used to being the brains of the operation so forgive me for asking questions. I am not used to a real man stepping up and taking charge."

"I told you baby girl I got you!" he said rubbing her face. Again, I know I was around most of them. I wanted this to be a complete surprise. I guarantee you will not regret it. Please let me make this special for you. Now stop asking questions."

She kissed him. Instantly, things get heated very quickly between them. Clothes began to unsnap and unzip. They contemplated if they should but the first and last time they had sexual relation was three months ago and they tried to rationalize one slip up. They tried to resist the urge but the feelings of being together drew them in deeper. It was more powerful than they could fight so they started to appease their flesh and figured on repenting later for yielding to the urges of temptation. Just as he was about to penetrate the phone rang. They ignored it and went back to the business at hand, but it rang again. Blue grabbed her phone and checked the caller ID. It was her mother. She knew something had to be wrong. She picked up the phone and called back.

"God always gives you an out!" Thank you Lord! she exhaled. "Hey Ma, what's wrong?"

"It is big mama. We had to rush her to the hospital. She just started having complications with her breathing and we couldn't figure out what was wrong with her, so we called the ambulance."

"Ok I am on the way home."

"No you don't have to come right now. But be on standby. She is not really talking. She is disoriented. The doctors are saying whatever this is does not look good especially for a woman her age."

"No Ma. I am coming home. I am on the way now!"

She hung up and is in a full panic. She tried to pack her bag, but she was majorly distressed. Mike held her hand and calmed her. She explained to him what her mother said about her grandmother. After she calmed down, she packed their bag and they left for the hospital. Mike called Don and explained the situation as he and Blue head for their destination. She cried frantically at the thought of losing her grandmother. He squeezed her hand and insisted she calmed down and tried not to upset herself or the baby. Blue and Mike arrived at the hospital.

They were pointed in the direction of her grandmother's room. Blue took a deep breath and walked in the door to see her grandmother lie there close to lifeless. She whimpered making way to her grandmother's bedside. She had never seen her grandmother so helpless.

She knew this was possible. She held Big Mama's hand and felt her grandmother try to squeeze her hand back. She could not contain her emotions and began to break down again. Mike stood beside her. She felt his arms wrap around her waist. He felt her stomach tighten. Losing Big Mama would be just as painful as losing her mother. Big mama was part of everything she knew. The family was called to gather to be with Big Mama. Waiting around her bedside they slowly began to talk about her and what a wonderful woman she was and how she had been the greatest impact in their lives. They talked about how she freely gave of herself not just to her family but to friends. She gave freely to her neighbors and even strangers. Big Mama was loved by all. Blue and Mama Bella were laughing when Celeste walked in.

She greeted everyone and tilted over to kiss and love on Big Mama. She slid Blue a chair and pointed for her to sit. The conversation continued as they waited on the doctor to finish with her test results. The wait seemed days long and she was declining before their eyes. The doctor walked in and began to run down a list of things that was wrong with their beloved Big Mama. He shook his head and assured them that she would not make it through the night, and they would keep her comfortable as she made her transition. The family began to take their time and slowly say their goodbyes to Big Mama. The clergyman came in and prayed with the family. Other friends and extended family members had been in and out.

Celeste stepped out to call Delmar and let him know what was going on. He gave his condolences and promised he and the kids would be with her first thing in the morning. He reassured her of his love, and they hung up. The family sat and talked and listened to the machines serving a reminder that Big Mama's time on earth with them would soon be coming to an end. Daylight took forever to come and as night slowly faded away so did the last breath from Big Mama. Celeste found herself in the arms of her husband. He caught her as she gave way to her emotions and wept for her adored matriarch. She had been their greatest teacher. She inspired so many. Most of all to them she was the world's greatest grandmother. Mike grabbed on to Blue and tried to comfort her as much as he could. He was allowing her to cry but tenderly reminded her that she had just gotten out of the hospital and she needed to think about her and the baby. He eased her out of the room to get some fresh air.

He went down to the cafeteria to pick up a couple of snacks for those who may have wanted something. He wanted to get food especially for Blue. She hadn't eaten and he needed to make sure she had something available. This was the first experience of death that had been this close to Blue. They weren't that close to their dad. When he died the impact was altered and the hurt was not as great. His wife oversaw everything, so they just had to show up and they were ok with that. But this time was different. Big Mama had been in their lives all their lives. They spent more time with her than with their mom. She treated Blue and Celeste more like daughters than granddaughters. The doctor gave his condolences and let them know the next steps to be taken and asked which funeral home would take the body. The hospital staff made proper phone calls to aid the family.

They took care of all they could at the hospital then went back to Big Mama's house and just sat and reminisced about the sassy mouthed, straight-no chaser God-fearing woman she was. The afternoon came and they all ventured to the funeral home and continued with planning the arrangements. Everyone was delegated jobs to make this a little bit easier for all involved. Blue had a gift with words, so she started writing the obituary. Once they left the funeral home she sat down and composed herself. She began to put her grandmother's mini bio on paper. Blue thought it would be most befitting to write a poem in honor of her Big Mama. She closed her eyes and said a prayer that God would allow her to pay tribute and homage to their beloved. She began to write, and the words flowed....

Big Mama, we thank God for you every day,
You taught us valuable lessons along life's journey way.
You were a woman, who stood on God's Holy word
All we had to do was listen and it could be heard.
You were a beautiful woman; to us you were as good as gold,
But if we struck a nerve, you would certainly get us told.
You were a virtuous woman known throughout the community,
You could always be found speaking peace, love, and unity.
You told us to be loving and kind to each other in your own
sweet voice.
But we knew we really didn't have any other choice.
You always said prayer is the key and faith unlocks the door.
Even in your leaving us we saw your testimony- and now we can
trust Christ more.
We saw Him keep you and sustain you and rock you in the
cradle of His love.
Now He has called you to rest in Heaven above.
You told us no matter how big or small- sin was still sin,
And don't take no wooden nickels- because they don't spend!
Wisdom like yours doesn't come anymore,

*It can't be found in a greeting card not even in the best
Hallmark store.
You would feed total strangers when in front of the house they
would pass,
We have seen you give your all right down to the very last.
You saw five generations and that is the number of Grace,
A part of you is in us all even down to the nose on our face!
You are not just gone see- we know just where you are,
You have gone to start your forever with our Heavenly
Father!!!!
The best part of it all is like you said, if we believe and trust in
Him as our Lord, Savior and Friend
Some sweet day Grandma we can rejoice because we will see
you again!!
We love you and take comfort in knowing you are resting in
Christ!!!
The Grands*

When she finished the poem she laid it down on the table. Celeste walked by and the poem caught her eye. She picked it up to read it and tears filled her eyes. She was speechless as she read the poem and noted how well Blue captured Big Mama in poetic form. She never doubted she could but to see it on paper made Big Mama's death a hard reality. She bent down to Blue and hugged her and rubbed her nephew. While they continued to make progress on the funeral arrangements Mike and Delmar checked on them periodically. Friends and extended family members showed their love and support by sending flowers and food. Some even sent monetary gifts. There was so much food taking up space it looked like "*big August meeting*" as Big Mama used to say.

That was how she described the yearly summer revival that happened in August. There was food coming from everywhere. One aunt's husband's family sent potato salad and green beans. Her other aunt's husband's family sent lima beans and a ham. The neighbor up the street sent a squash and a broccoli casserole. Mike's mom made several cakes and pies. The missionaries brought in sodas and tea. Other auxiliaries of the church brought in lemonade and cases of water. The food kept coming over the next several days. They had so much food it was requested to have the food taken to the fellowship hall of the church for the repass.

It was the day of Big Mama's homegoing service. Nerves were all over the place as they paid their final respects to the woman who (by the help of the good Lord) had been their everything for the past years. They wept tears of sorrow and some of joy throughout the service. Listening to all the beautiful cards and remarks being made about their cherished love one gave them comfort in knowing that she was well loved by all. The preacher preached a most encouraging message and once he finished it was time to view their Big Mama for the last time. The morticians ushered for all to come and get one last look at Big Mama as she laid there in the beautiful blue casket with a hue of grey. She had a peace that covered her in her transition.

She laid there in a very uninterrupted and tranquil rest. Her skin carried the same glow it had when she was alive. Even though she laid there lifeless she looked as though time had stopped and reset her back thirty years. She died at the sweet old age of ninety- four but didn't look a day over sixty-three. Finally that part was over. That was the hardest part of all, watching them close the lid and saying the final goodbye, knowing it was forever- at least on this side of heaven. They gather up her flowers to put at the gravesite and listened as they committed Big Mama to the ground. Afterwards they released doves then went inside for the repass.

"I can't eat any more bird! Between mama's pre-Thanksgiving meal, all this repass food and Thanksgiving being around the corner, I don't want another home cooked meal until next year," Blue whispered loudly.

"Me either, but you need to eat. You are pregnant and you have been picking at every meal for the past two days. So eat all of something babe please," Mike pleaded.

"Dear God, if I never see a green bean again in the next six months it will be too soon, I could go for a greasy steak and cheese sub and some fries," Delmar joked.

"Yeeeeeeeessssss!" they all yelled.

"I promise I won't cook another bean until you ask for them!" she winked. "The service was nice, and it was a huge crowd. Big Mama was loved by many. She lived a good long life. I wish these little people could know her the way we did and got a chance to be spoiled by her," Celeste added.

"Yea I know. If you didn't know her then you missed a treat because she was a trip," Blue smiled.

"Wasn't she?! Lord have mercy… That lady! That lady! That lady!" Ms. Bella chimed in as she walked over to the four of them.

The family began to laugh. They knew exactly what was meant in those two words. They made ready to depart from the place where they laid the much-loved queen of their hearts. When they got back to the house

Blue broke the news to her mother that she and Mike were going to leave. They said their goodbyes and planned to see each other in a few weeks for Christmas. Blue thought about it and became sad. She started a new chapter in her life and Big Mama was no longer around to see it. She only had memories and photos of Big Mama to pass down to baby Kristopher. He would only have stories of the woman who had a loving helping hand in molding her into the woman she was. She only hoped the stories she'd tell would do justice to describe the woman she was.

Mike and Blue said their goodbyes and made way back home. While Mike drove Blue dozed off and had a nice long nap on the ride. A few miles from the house Mike began to rub Blue's leg to wake her. He desperately wanted access to her girl part. He wanted her to open her legs more and give him complete contact. He yearned to be in her most inner part. He remembered how it felt and how her body answered his call their first encounter. He imagined her being freshly waxed and tucked away all nice and warm. That turned Mike on. Mike swore his imagination was gonna get him in trouble. He promised to be different. With his hand rested on her leg he fought the visuals of them in his head and moved his hand and softly caressed her face.

"Mmmmmmmmmm."

"Wake up baby, it is time to go in the house. We are here."

"What a way to wake up."

"I can tell you that is not really what I wanted to do. You had your thighs all out looking tasty this whole ride. I had to meditate on the Lord. Girl you turn me on. I know we have vowed for me to keep my snake out of your grass, but what about my hand."

"You are out of control. What about your hand? This is why I love you; you have the best sense of humor!" she laughed.

"I am going to get the bags out of the car." he shrugged.

"No sir! Baby that can wait until morning."

"Uuuuh ok if you say so!"

They ran into the house and undressed and crawled in Blue's bed for a change of scenery. Mike laid on Blue's lap and watched television. Blue picked her Bible up from the nightstand and put it across her chest. It was the one her grandmother gave her when she went off to college. She remembered how she'd flipped through it and found a few hundred-dollar bills throughout it. Mike got hungry and went in the kitchen and made them a snack. Blue laid in bed and waited for Mike to finish. She thought of her wedding day and how it could not come fast enough. After their one sexual encounter she did want more of him.

She anxiously wanted him inside her body again. She had never experienced anyone like Mike Long, and she was excited that she would get to experience him for the rest of her lifetime. He came back in the bedroom with a bowl of ice cream. Mike handed Blue her spoon. Blue got a little bit of ice cream on her finger. Mike licked it off. As she continued to eat she purposely let ice cream fall off the spoon and land on her chest. Mike licked the ice cream off her chest. He kissed her neck then placed his lips on hers. Mike fed her a cherry. Blue sucked the cherry residue off his finger.

"Shoot babe you need to go and get your dress ASAP. I am ready to make love to you on a regular. I have everything ready to go. I just need the day to hurry up and get here. I need to mold your body to mine."

"I know. I never thought I would see you in this light but now that I do. I want to be near you. I could always wrap myself around you. The feelings I feel for you Mike Long are intense. I love the smell of you. I love the feel of you. I love the taste of your lips and breathing you in when we kiss. I love you."

"I love you too and I will say it again. I have loved you since the first day I laid eyes on you."

"Uuuuuuuuuugh! When are we going to make this official?"

"The day I tell you to get your beautiful self-dressed. I shall have you picked up and delivered to the desired destination."

Blue looked down at her belly and sighed. She lifted her shirt. As she rubbed her belly and noticed her stomach has begun to show several dark and light lines of growth.

"He is definitely real now. I see the growing and the stretching of my belly. I hope I can bounce back from this experience. Babies can jack your body up. Lawd."

"You are beautiful and there is nothing wrong with you or your body. I love your belly, it's where my babies will come from."

He kissed her chin, and she kissed his forehead. They smiled.

"Mike if I hadn't said it I say it now. Thank you for loving me with someone else's child. This is not my ideal situation, but I am glad we can make the best of it."

"Girl! I keep telling you I love all of you and this child. I am all in. He is part of you. I know the situation behind it. You didn't cheat on me and get pregnant. It was something that happened before we discovered our feelings for each other. Blue you have to forgive yourself. We didn't know about the baby. It is my pleasure and privilege to love you. It is an honor and my duty to care for you and provide for us. Now come on and let's get my son in the bed. You have a long day ahead of you tomorrow going back to work and all. Are you up to that?"

"Yea bae I can handle it. Thanks. Hey and you know what?"

"What's that beautiful?"

"It is a privilege and pleasure to love you as well. I count it an honor to be Mrs. Long and make this house our home. I have never been swept off my feet like this before and if this is what dying and going to heaven is like then I look forward to forever dying daily. I could get lost in you Mike."

"Love, I am already lost in you."

He pulled the covers and laid down beside her, prayed over her and waited for her to fall sleep. She laid there and thanked her God for being merciful and gracious enough to send Mike to love her. She was still pleasantly surprised at how it all came together. Mike was in the business of spoiling his women to a certain extent. However, the one he made a vow to, he promised to give her as much of the world as he could with no questions asked- no bars held. After Blue fell asleep Mike got up and left for the lounge.

Chapter 7

Sunday was a busy night for the lounge. He wanted and needed to show his face. He walked in, spotted a young lady he knew from his hometown. She was known for letting anyone or anything with a second head have a chance with her. At one point she had it bad for Mike and he knew it. He steered clear of her because she was the type of woman his daddy strongly advised not to bring home. They exchanged greetings and she is excited to find out that Mike has come to the big city and done what she thought was well for himself. He had hoped she had changed. Maybe become a born-again virgin or something or maybe settled with a family of her own.

He could tell that was not the case. She was married but changed she had not. Her husband thought he could change her and finally wised up. As the associate pastor of one of the local congregations, he could not afford to continue to put himself or his girls through the effects of her lifestyle any longer. He left her and took their two daughters. He loved her, but it wasn't enough. He hoped she would change on her own or at least try for the girls. It hurt him but he knew he could not allow his daughters to become products of their mother or risk them exhibiting the same ungodly behaviors. It was clear she was on the prowl and she was wanting Mike to be her next victim.

"So, this is your spot?" she queried.

"Yes ma'am it is," he answered.

"I love it. There is nothing else like this in this neck of the woods. You were always a smart man. I liked and admired that about you when we were in school," she continued. "You were always very quiet too. If I faintly recall correctly."

"Yeah I know, thanks. I did my research. I spoke as needed and to whom when needed."

She reached her hand towards his face. He moved and entertained her a few minutes more. She took a sip of her drink and mustard up the courage to expose her intent. It was a moment she had always hoped for.

"What, you can't handle a woman like me Mike. Huh? You scared?"

"Nope! Look I am off the market and I have a beautiful fiancé who is pregnant with our son waiting at home for me. I am flattered but I am simply NOT interested. But on the bright side I am sure another sucker I mean guy in here would be."

He ordered her a drink on the house and walked away. He indistinctly heard her mumble something under her breath. He shook his head and chuckled while he walked through greeting his guests. She licked her wombs and moved right along to the next man. Hours passed and it is time for the lounge to close. Mike and Don closed out the tabs and registers. The staff began to clean and restock. They prepared items for lunch hours the next day. Just as the sun came up Mike walked in the house. He went in Blue's room and nudged her neck to wake her. He greeted her with the sweetest morning kiss. She rolled over and rubbed his head and face. He whispered, "Good morning." They have brief conversation before she showered and dressed for work. He fixed her breakfast. She hurried and ate her food, kissed him, and rushed out to work. She couldn't wait to get back to her office. She missed her patients.

"Goooooooooooooood morning boss lady welcome back!" She was cheerfully greeted by her staff. They had cards and balloons waiting for her to let her know that she was loved and missed for the past two and a half weeks and they stood behind and supported her.

"Lil girl," she heard a voice call. "How are you feeling?" Ms. Deb inquired.

"I am good. From the bottom of my heart thank you for being there for me always, especially these past few weeks. With being in the hospital with the baby and Big Mama passing I honest to God appreciate you. I also appreciate Mr. Jim and the kids."

"Baby girl, you are welcome. When I broke the news to the kids about your grandmother child, they got all beside themselves. They have been wanting to come and spend some time with you. I told them they need to wait until you felt up to it."

"Aww how sweet. I will make plans this weekend to have them over to the house so they can spend time with us. Maybe we will make pizzas and watch a movie. Mike has a projector and a big popcorn machine in the movie room he is dying to use. We don't go in there so he will absolutely love that.

Her first day back was the busiest to her it seemed. She felt like she had patients everywhere, but she and her staff got it done. They all praised each other for an awesome day's work and agreed to see each other tomorrow. Blue pulled out of her office driveway. She noticed a black Mercedes pull out with her. She didn't get too worked up until it started to follow her. When she turned, so did the other car. She became nervous. She rode the car right past the police station and began to turn in to park. The car sped off in the other direction. She sat there for a minute. An officer noticed her and asked if she needed assistance?

She explained what she thought happened. He offered to follow her home. On the drive home she called Mike and explained to him what happened and for him not to be alarmed because she was ok. She pulled up in the driveway. Mike stood on the porch waiting for her. She opened the garage and pulled the jeep in. The officer parked and met Blue and Mike in the yard. They thanked him over and over for his service, he handed them his card and left. Mike embraced her and made sure she was ok. She promised him she was. They walked in the house. He grabbed his cell and made a call.

"Ok yes sir. Will do. Alright peace. That was my boy. On your lunch break tomorrow, we are going to sign you up for a conceal weapons class. While you wait to take the class, we are going to the gun range."

"Mike that is not necessary. I am ok and I don't like guns."

"Yea I hear you but hear me. I can't be with you 24/7, as much as I would like to that just is not possible. I could hire someone to keep tabs on you, but we all know you would hate that worse than hemorrhoids. My only option is to teach you how to protect yourself with a weapon. I pray to God you never have to use it. I don't like this mess Blue. We already know who it is and why. If he comes around here, I will be certain to finish what he started. Blue I'm not a killer but he is pushing me. I will defend mine at all costs. You keep talking about his career, but I don't give two turds about any of that. He is posing a threat to you and I don't like it. Honestly, why do you think he won't kill again. He is a murderer Blue be it accidently or on purpose." he reminded her.

"Mike that was different. He was protecting his sister," she said.

"Are you serious? Are you defending this dude?" he asked.

"No babe. I am just trying to make sense of it all as well. I don't want to get all worked up over nothing. Bae calm down please." she begged.

She pulled him close and rubbed his back and arms. He turned around and held on to her like it was the last time he would see her. She tried to wiggle her way out of his grip, but she could not. She teased him about his tight hold he had on her. She tried to break the tension that they allowed to come between them with the past lover. They sat down to dinner and continued to discuss their day. She inquired about him not going to culinary school since his passion for food was inevitable. He explained to her that his mother went, and she taught him everything she knew about cooking and as he got older he added his own twist and style on the foods she taught him and liked to create some meals of his own. They joked about his father not being able to boil water. His dad was raised with his mom and sisters and made a home with a woman who could cook so he never had reason to learn. Mike's mom always had some type of prepared meal in the freezer so if she had to go away without him, he wouldn't be hungry.

Blue confessed that her mother taught her how to cook as well but she was not fond of doing so. She was simply happy with just being the taste tester then being called to eat. She didn't think she needed that survival skill, but she learned in protest how to cook and she was able to keep herself from going hungry. Blue ushered Mike to the table and began to plate their food since he cooked. Mike stood at the door of the living room and watched the game. Being overtaken by a pain Blue yelled out. Scared, Mike ran over to her and tried to aid in her dilemma. She just moaned with no words. Unsure of what to do, he broke out in a prayer and a cold sweat as he stood there waiting for her to say something that would allow him to help her. In between breaths she managed to tell him the baby's movements are horribly painful. He sat her down and they rub him back into a central location. Baby Kristopher fought but finally complied with them. Her pain soon subsided, and they sat down to dinner.

They dimmed the lights and lit candles for the table. Mike turned on the radio and they sat and ate dinner and enjoyed the company of each other. After dinner, Mike decided to take Blue out for ice cream. They talked about attending the baby shower for her future goddaughter and reminded Mike about Thanksgiving dinner at Ms. Deb's. Mike agreed. It would be good for them to stay in town close to home due to all they had endured over the past few weeks. It was time for Blue to go back to her doctor. Her doctor was adamant about seeing her on a biweekly basis since the incident. On their way back to the house Coco called. They only spoke briefly. Blue was informed that Coco's father-in-law fell ill, and the in-laws could no longer plan the baby shower and pleaded for Blue to come to her aid. Coco told her she knew it was short notice and asked her to take over. The shower invitations had been sent and the cake had been ordered. There was only a matter of food and decorations.

Blue volunteered Mike for food. She essentially needed paper goods, a few balloons, and some cute tabletop decorations. They brainstormed about games they could play. The event would be held in Coco's home and Rod would be available to be of service if she needed. The baby was due any day now. The shower was only a few days away. Blue accepted the challenge for her best friend. On the way back to the house Blue told Mike what she had agreed them to. Mike looked at her and shook his head.

She smiled nervously. They arrived back home and go inside, Mike sat down for a minute then dressed for work. On the way out the door he kissed her and set the alarm. He made a phone call for his homeboy Rick to come over and add extra cameras around the house just to be on the safe side. He couldn't remember if Terrance knew where he lived. He wanted to be sure to catch any kind of potential stupidity. Mike called a few of his friends that he knew kept late hours and asked them ride by and check on the house. He was not taking any chances.

His job was to protect her and keep her safe and that was what he intended to do. He planned to love and shield her as Christ loved the church and that meant laying down his life if he had to. Mike finished at the lounge and went home to his favorite girl. He tried to come in quietly but to his surprise Blue was already in his bed waiting on him. She explained she missed him, and she just wanted to be next to his belongings. She slid over and he joined her on the bed. She made her way into his arms and on his chest. She listened to the solid beat of his heart as he breathed, she began to breathe the same rhythmic pattern. She laid there in comfort and complete security and she slept until the sun greeted her with a gentle kiss and her alarm blared. She eased out of his arms, walked in her room, and dressed for work. She walked back in Mike's room to kiss him goodbye only to find him putting his shoes on and grabbing his keys.

He decided he would be taking her to work and picking her up until he felt comfortable they were not going to be harassed anymore. She promised him she could take care of herself and she would be fine but by then his mind was made up and he was done listening. She reminded him about her doctor's appointment during her lunch and he agreed to come back and get her when it was time. There was no escaping it.

This was happening. She pleaded with him that all of this was not necessary, but he just looked at her as he picked up the keys and pointed. She grabbed her lunch and pouted out of the door. Laughing at her, he gave her a choice of his ride or hers. She slow walked to the passenger side of her car and flopped in. Mike found her temper tantrum hilarious. On the drive to work he stopped and picked her up breakfast. Mike laughed at her as she sat and sulked the whole ride. She understood his care but felt it unnecessary. She loved that he cared, but she felt this was overboard. She tried to be mad, but she knew his heart was in the right place. They arrived at her place of work and she tried to assure him one last time this was not needed.

Mike looked at her with an "I am not going to say it again look." She dropped her head in surrender and stuck her forehead out to be kissed. She walked tail tucked in the building as she felt some type of way. The more she thought about it the more she secretly loved that he loved her in that way. She smirked to herself and her heart fluttered as she turned around and watched him drive off. She walked in the door. As Blue came in with her lip poked out she ran into Ms. Deb. She inquired about the long sad face. Blue began telling Ms. Deb how Mike dropped her off at work this morning due to the suspicions of a potential Big siting. She replayed last evening after work. She promised Ms. Deb that Mike was being irrational. Blue continued to tell her side of the story looking for a cosigner, but she misread the sign because Ms. Deb was not agreeing to anything on her behalf. She reminded Blue of what she'd been through over the past several weeks and how stress was not good for her or what she needed. Ms. Deb gave her a few more words of encouragement and then they began to discuss the Thanksgiving meal.

Ms. Deb was so proud of herself. She was to prepare the entire meal and was only asking that her family come and enjoy. Thanksgiving was Mr. Jim's project, but this year she figured she would give him a break. She ran down her menu of traditional favorites-turkey, ham, fried chicken, her famous yams, corn, and green beans. She mentioned fresh greens and chitterlings. She began to plan her week and how she would need to prep and cook everything if she were going to have it all done by Thanksgiving.

She rambled on about the macaroni and cheese along with the corn bread being the last thing she would pull out of the oven right before everyone arrived. Blue tuned back in when she began to talk about the pound cake, carrot cake and the sweet potato pies. Besides her mother's, Ms. Deb's dessert recipes could be put in a book and published. She could cook, but baking was her specialty. Blue promised to eat all she could and thanked Ms. Deb in advance for not judging her for how she would freely enjoy those desserts. Blue mentioned to her the baby shower and the ideas she had thus far with it being short notice.

The day passed and they laughed and joked as they worked. Blue felt a little better about the driving arrangement but then again, she really didn't have a choice. The nurse came in with a dozen roses. She smiled and cooed and informed Blue she would sit them on her desk. Confused she wondered who in the world sent them. She knew she'd left Mike in a little funk, but it didn't warrant flowers. She finished up with her patient and walked in her office. She walked over to her desk and looked at the card. It read, *"Just something to brighten your day."* She sat at her flowers and began to shake.

The more she looked at them and who they came from the angrier she became. Ms. Deb began to worry and went to her office to check on her. Ms. Deb walked and found Blue slamming the flowers in the garbage. Blue handed Ms. Deb the note and dropped her head. Ms. Deb read the note and sighed. She asked Blue did she think Mike was overreacting now that there are flowers from her ex sitting in the trash. Blue wasn't sure how she was gonna handle the situation, but she knew she couldn't tell Mike about the flowers. She needed think time, but she didn't have long. Mike was coming to get her at lunch for her appointment. She couldn't go to the police; she felt she had no grounds to stand on.

She was stuck and could not figure her way out of it. She figured she would make it through the day then figure out something from there. In her throw, she'd broken the vase. Blue cleaned up the excess flowers and cut her had on a piece of the broken glass. It wasn't stitch worthy, but it was definitely noticeable. Ms. Deb handed

Blue a bandage from her cabinet and helped her finish cleaning up the mess. Blue breathed in and out trying to calm herself. She could not let this ruin her day. She saw her last two patients for that morning and waited for Mike. He pulled up right on schedule. He watched their surroundings. He opened the door and put her in the car. Still mad from the flowers she tried to hide her anger and pretend all was well. They kissed and she sighed in relief to be in his presence.

"Hey beautiful! How has your day been so far?" he asked.

"It's been ok," she shrugged.

"Ok. You alright?" he asked.

"I will be," she shrugs again.

What is going on with you and why all the shrugging shoulders, what happened to your hand?" he prods.

"It is nothing," she insisted. "Can we just drop it please?"

He drove a little farther down the street and they sat quiet with nothing but the radio going which was just loud enough to drown out her thoughts. It still wasn't enough to keep her confession to herself. She couldn't bear the reason of her tension from him any longer. She took a deep breath and let it out.

"Today I got flowers," she began. "From Terrance," she said apprehensively.

She anticipated Mike to blow his top. She braced herself for it. She didn't expect him to remain calm. Mike nodded as he listened. He couldn't believe how persistent guy was. He thought dude had to be glutton for punishment. Something had to be done about this. Big had to be stopped.

"Oh he did, did he?" he continued.

With her eyes wide in disbelief she asked, "So you are not mad?"

"Oh hell yeah. I am mad. Pretty pissed off. I don't need to let you see that side of me because it is going to stress you out and considering what you have just recovered from there is nothing to be solved by yelling and carrying on. It is going to be ok. You just let me worry about ole' boy. Don't stress it love. I got you." he nodded.

She felt better knowing that she had gotten that off her chest. She didn't know what he was going to do or how, but she felt comfortable and trusted him. They arrived at the doctor's office. She signed in at the desk and waited for them to call her back. As they sat and waited she noticed Mike was not as jumpy as he once was coming to the visits. She assumed it was because he was too preoccupied thinking about the whole Big situation to focus on being skittish while in there. They called Blue and Mike back and had Blue give a urine sample. She weighed in and had her pressure taken. When they finished it was off to the ultrasound room to see baby Kristopher. She got undressed and the sonographer began. They listen to his strong heartbeat. Mike took his cell phone and recorded it. Blue just watched him and fell in love with him all over again. He put his phone away.

It looked as if he were waving as she measured his

body and the circumference of his little head. They also received confirmation that the name Kristopher was still a go. They collected the ultrasound pictures of baby Kristopher. For a moment, they forgot about the real world and all that was in it. Nothing mattered past what was in that room right then and there. They were instructed to wait in the seating area for the doctor to see her. Mike helped her off the table. She wiped off and got dressed. The doctor came in and they all talked. He asked Blue a round of questions and she answered.

She assured the doctor she would do all she could to keep calm and stay stress free. She mentioned that the only stress in her life right now was good stress and how she was excited about planning a baby shower for her best friend and future godchild. The doctor placed the charge on Mike to make sure she was to remain calm. Mike assured the doctor he had the same plans for her in mind along with some vacation and spa time in between. They checked out. Mike grabbed Blue a bite to eat and took her back to work. They returned to her office. He opened the door for her and in her ear he whispered, "I love you." She took in his scent and whispered back, "I love you more." He checked their surroundings and walked her to the door.

They kissed like they may never get the chance to again. She walked in her building and he pulled off. Ms. Deb greeted her at the door with questions. Blue answered the questions in the order they were asked. She mentioned to Ms. Deb that she informed Mike about the flowers and although he stayed calm, he was not happy in the least, but it didn't solve anything by being all mad and unruly.

Blue gave a detailed run down of her doctor's appointment. She sighed as she thought about her Big problem and how she was going to get him to go away especially when he made it more than clear that he didn't want anything to do with her or her son. Ms. Deb gave her a great big mama bear hug and a few more words of encouragement and told her to get back to work. Blue thanked Ms. Deb and let her know her words were appreciated.

She sat at her desk, picked up her phone and looked up abortion clinics. She blamed herself for not thinking of this out sooner, but in her defense, she didn't know Big would be acting the way he was. She knew she was too far along to have one, but the idea still seemed like a good one. She thought about giving the child up for adoption but that wouldn't make him go away either. She felt her baby move and put her phone down. She begged God for forgiveness for the thoughts that just went through her head. That wasn't what she wanted but she felt she had no way out. She remembered that it didn't matter how the baby came to be, but he was a gift from God and if she had to deal with Big for the next 18 years then so be it. That was simply the cross she would have to bear. The more she got to know her son the more she fell in love with him. She couldn't see under any circumstances giving him up or getting rid of him.

Blue allowed a few tears to stream down her face. Then pulled it together. She rubbed her baby. There was a bakery few doors down everyone loved. Blue called in an order of sweet treats and had them delivered to her staff as a token of appreciation for how hard they'd worked. She poured herself into her work for the next few hours and tried not to think about her current situation. Finally it was time to go home. They closed the office, and everyone said their goodbyes. Mike stood with her door open waiting on her. She greeted him with a kiss. He waved and blew a kiss at Ms. Deb and reiterated them seeing her on Thursday afternoon. They drove home in silence. Enough had already been said. Blue could not help but wonder what was going on in Mike's mind. They pulled into the house to find an unfamiliar truck.

"Oh that's Rick, I told you he was coming to upgrade the security system. I am having cameras added in different locations of the house too," he reminded her.

"Oh yeah. Now I remember," she said.

They got out of the car. She and Rick exchange hellos and she went in the house. She drug her tired body to the bathroom for a shower. She put her lounge clothes on, sat down on the couch and relaxed. Mike tried to make peace and brought her a cup of hot chocolate the way she liked it with milk and extra marshmallows. He mentioned his parents sent their love from the phone call earlier in the day.

"Hey," he said. "What time is the baby shower Saturday?"

"It is at 2:00. Why, what do you have in mind?"

"Well nothing now for this weekend. That is right in the middle of the day and you ladies are not going to be finished before late. Since you voluntold me to bring the food I needed to know what time and what I am preparing so I will have everything ready on my end. Do I have to be there the whole time?"

He sat down beside her and put her feet in his lap. He poured lotion in his hands and begin to rub her feet and legs. Her reaction revealed his hands were magic and relaxing to the touch. She closed her eyes and just as he made way to massage her inner thigh the doorbell rang.

"Dang it boy," she shouted.

Mike laughed at her and shook his head. "Baby I will be right back to pick up where I left off."

"You better," she mumbled.

He answered the door. Rick let him know he was finished and was ready to explain all the additional bells and whistles they added to their alarm. They came back in and have a seat. Mike wrapped his arm around Blue as they talk. He looked at her then kissed her on the forehead. She closed her eyes and inhaled. Rick finished the presentation. He downloaded the app to their phones and showed them how to navigate it. They exchange a few more words and he walked toward the door. Mike went in the room and came back with payment. Rick showed Mike everything he'd added on the house and how far the view on the cameras extended. He assured him that the system was top of the line and the sound could be picked up from the edge of his yard. Mike inquired about Rick's new Jamaican lady friend that he met a few months back. Rick noted that he was just as happy as Mike and Blue were and they had the potential to be serious. Mike encouraged him to hang in there and hoped she was the one.

They talked a little more as Rick downloaded the app for the security system to their phones and showed them how to use it. When they finished Mike invited Rick and his new lady to the lounge for the VIP experience on him.

Rick called his girl to tell her the news. She was excited. She'd tried to make reservations for months and could never get in because it was booked. Rick let her know he and Mike were friends and he didn't want to divulge that information until they were serious. Rick finished giving Mike the overview of the system and left.

Mike closed the door behind Rick. He stood at the door a few minutes and played with the alarm then walked back over to the couch and continued where he left off. He picked up her feet and begun to rub them again. He traveled from her feet to her legs then up to the inner parts of her thighs. She closed her eyes and concentrated on the touch of his hands and how they made her feel. She thought briefly for a moment on how she was a fool. She could have been enjoying Mike Long in his entirety and already have kids in elementary school.

Life would have been so much simpler. She would not be going through any of these unnecessary changes. It wasn't her ideal situation to be in. She took a deep breath and began to bask in Mike's special treatment of her. She knew the love was genuine and the man would move mountains for her or at least try his hardest to. He rubbed her thighs and she rubbed on his back and head. She found herself inching up closer to him until she was straddled his lap. They kissed and caressed each other. She began to massage his shoulders. The more they rubbed and kissed the more excited they became. They tried to hold out but couldn't any longer.

Mike moved his body with hers. He ran his hands down her back and into her shorts. He rubbed and caressed her body. She moaned to his touch. She moved her body on his. She wished and hoped they would lose control and make love once more, then get serious about their celibacy until they were officially married.

"You sure you want to do this? We have our first premarital counseling session with Pastor Williams tomorrow," he reminded her.

"Baby I won't tell if you don't," she replied with one eyebrow lifted.

He stared at her for a while. He zoned out and began to think of what making love to her again would be like. He imagined he pulled her as close as he could to him, caressing her body to prepare her for a round of him. He spread out a blanket laid her down on the floor and went and grabbed a towel. He drug his tongue from her neck to her nipples and listened to her moan in pleasure and anticipation of what was soon to follow. He grabbed the message oil and took his time to rub and caress her. He ran his tongue again around the sacred parts of her body. His fingers found their way into her hello kitty. They enter having a few moments of exploration. Her muscles tightened and her movements were quickened as she released herself.

She whimpered as she lost control of herself in him. He smiled as he is watched her enjoy the climax. He put a pillow under her and turned her on her side. She arched her body in preparation for his entrance. She inhaled and waited until he was inside her to release. She cried out in both pleasure and pain. She reached back for his head as he grabbed her waist and began to give her the long, strong yet gentle thrusts of his man part. She straddled her legs as wide as she could across him and received him again. He thrusted up and down under her as his hands rested on her waist. She put her hands in his and they climaxed together.

"Mike! Mike hello, where did you go?"

"Oh I am sorry. I just made love to you in my head," he admitted.

"Without me! Dang. That's messed up! I am sitting here a willing participant."

"My bad. It is better that way for now. This is hard!"

She mushed his face and climbed off his lap. They laid in the floor and Mike told Blue of the fantasy he'd had in his mind. Blue mentioned that this weekend she was going to start looking for a cute little dress to marry him in. She wanted him not to make a big deal out of them getting married.

Chapter 8

She made him promise that it would only be just immediate friends and family. While Blue went on Mike laid there and played in her hair. He smiled as she rambled on knowing he had already prearranged everything and was waiting on the day to come to execute his plan. Even though they were getting married Christmas day he and Celeste had already had conversation about everything, including the setup.

She'd planned to arrive a few days early to help Mike bring everything else together. She would lay low and out of site at Ms. Deb's. The next few weeks would be deemed unforgettable. He tuned back in and agreed to everything she said. He reassured her he was listening. He knew Blue wanted to be a wife before she was a mother. So he figured that was the best gift he could give her on Christmas day. He thought it to be an honor to grant her request. He called her doctor for clearance on her traveling as well. He booked them a flight and a seven-day honeymoon to Aruba. They would bring in the New Year as man and wife on a nice warm resort.

Her passport had many travel miles but none that lead there. With everything that had happened so far, the honeymoon would be a much-needed vacation for them both. Mike reached over and turned up the volume on the radio. He heard an ole school love song he hadn't heard in a long time. He lipped the words to her as he was not vocally blessed either. He jumped remembering his surprise for her. He ran to the room and came back. He instructed her to hold out her hand and close her eyes. He placed her hand on the bag and she opened her eyes. She reached in the bag and pulled out a kid's baseball bat with the ball and glove.

She looked it over and noticed the glove had been initialed KML and there were unidentified signatures on the ball and bat. She noticed one special autograph on it. It read, *to my Godson Kristopher, love Uncle Chuck.* Mike's childhood friend played on his favorite baseball team. Chuck was a gifted baseball player drafted right out of his first year of college. He and his teammates signed the items to the new baby. Blue began to cry hysterically. She could not believe Mike had that done. She tried to figure out when he even had the time.

"Oh my God Mike this is incredible. I love it so much...aww my God," she cried.

"I hope you didn't mind I picked his new godfather. Chuck loves the Lord; everyone loves him, and he has a great influence and impact in the community. I know you remember us hanging out with him and his wife a few times. You know his first born is my goddaughter. She is getting ready to graduate high school. I don't see her as much as I used to cause she is driving and busy with school and sports. Uncle Mike has been on the back burner. We call each other and I try to make it to her games. She is one of the best on the softball field like her old man and she is smart. She already has a full ride to NYU. She also let me know she needed a job for the summer. She wants to work at the new place."

"No baby I don't mind at all. We have been friends for over eight years, I trust your judgement and yes Chuck is a wonderful man. We are honored to have him as godfather. I remember her a little. She used to be with you all the time. I wondered what happened to her. She is the one who used to make her parents call you to come get her."

"Right," he agreed.

Mike told Blue of his plans to open the new restaurant and gaming center. Blue put him on pause and hurriedly ran and put the baby's things in his room on top of his mounted wall shelf right under his name. On her way back she detoured for the bathroom. She came back and sat on the couch. Mike laid his head in her lap. She rubbed his head and they continued to talk. He revealed the name of the restaurant. Blue jumped up with excitement accidently pushing Mike to the floor. She quickly gathered herself and apologized. She never imagined her kid's name on the side of his own business. As with everything else, God used Mike as a vessel, and he was making it happen. He continued to describe the restaurant as a kid friendly establishment and when baby Kristopher was older he could do what he wanted with the property. Mike teased about him making it a strip club if he chose.

Blue looked at him. Mike laughed and guaranteed her it was a place for kids to safely come, eat, play, and enjoy themselves. He highlighted his favorite part was the outside batting cage. It has everything he wished they had in a restaurant as kids and then some. Blue shared in his excitement. She warned that any other children they have may be pissed that their oldest sibling had a business in his name. Mike assured what he did for one he would do for the others. He already had ideas and plans in motion for any other children they would have. Mike was big on creating wealth for his family. He had it good as a child, but he desired better for his children.

Unaware of the time they continued to talk until they heard their stomachs growl. They agreed to pizza and Mike called out for it. Blue made a salad while they waited for the food to arrive. The phone and doorbell rang at the same time. Mike grabbed the door and Blue answered the phone.

"Hello. Hey Pastor Williams. How are you? No, no sir you are not disturbing anything. We're ready and excited about our first counseling session. Ok great, you said 5:30 tomorrow afternoon right? We will see you then."

She hung up and over dinner explained to Mike that Pastor Williams wanted to confirm their meeting for tomorrow. They continued to eat. When finished they moved the conversation back to the living room. It was bedtime. They said their goodnights and went into their own rooms. Blue looked back at him and shook her head, still in disbelief that she was so close to making love to him and missed the opportunity.

The next morning Mike took Blue to work again against her wishes. She protested silently but she knew it was not worth the fight to say anything out loud. She grabbed her yogurt and her lunch he packed her and waddled herself to the passenger side of the car. Work went by fast and the day seemed like it did not take long to end. Ms. Deb hit the alarm and they dispersed to their vehicles heading in their own direction. Mike inquired about Blue's day. She responded as it being a little hectic and busy but for the most part pretty good. At 5:25 they arrived at the church. Mike looked up in the rear-view mirror and saw Pastor Williams pull up right behind him.

"Good evening my brother and sister in the Lawd," he greeted them.

"Hey pastor Williams," they both greeted him.

They exchanged handshakes and hugs and did some small talk on the way to his office. They sat down around his table and Pastor Williams opened their meeting with prayer.

"I understand you want to be married soon. Is it because Kristen is already pregnant?" he asked.

"We do because we love each other, not because I am pregnant," Kristen explained dropping her head.

"Hold your head up now. Things happen! You must repent and seek God for forgiveness. You must give an account to Him not to me. I neither condemn nor condone. My job is to proclaim God's gospel and His standards and let Him deal with you accordingly. For the Bible says, "you must work out your own salvation with fear and trembling." That means it is between you and God. Now Mike and Kristen, you want to get married? Let's go to God's word and see what He says about it," he eases the tension with a smile.

The counseling session went on for what appeared to be hours. It was an intense and real eye opener. Pastor Williams went on to ask them a series of questions and then referenced multiple scriptures for answers. They had to explain to him the situation of Blue being pregnant and it not being Mike's. They also had to divulge the whole living situation agreement. There was some crying and quite a bit of laughter. Most of all there were some cold hard truths being listed inside those four walls. But together they were willing to accept those truths and move forward. He also told them that since they wanted him to marry them soon then they needed to meet at least two more times for him to be satisfied with performing their marriage ceremony. He gave them homework and expected it to be done.

He let them know that if they are having any type of premarital sex that it should be stopped, and they need to commit themselves to really hearing what the Lord had to say to each of them. He told them that he had watched them grow as members in his church. He knew that it was a matter of time before the two best friends became something more. He closed the meeting with prayer and assured the couple they would be just fine. He heavily persuaded them to continue to have some restraint. They agreed they had and would continue. They thanked the pastor and said their goodbyes. They grabbed a bit to eat and went home.

"Oh my God! Pastor Williams is no joke!" Blue exhaled.

"No he is not. But I figured that going in. We got work to do but we knew that too. It is not like a big surprise or anything. I am really glad now I made love to you in my head last night."

"Don't remind me. We got to get serious about this. These almost slips can't keep happening either."

"We got it. We can do this," Mike assured.

"I thought he was going to go in on me when I told him about our situation."

"Why would he, he is a man, and we all make mistakes. I like that he understands."

"Yea me too. He doesn't condemn or condone. He speaks to God's standard and not his."

They went in the house. They remembered what the pastor told them, kissed each other on the cheek and went to their rooms for the night. They got up the next day and it was business as usual. Mike dropped Blue off at work then came back at closing time and picked her up. They went home and Mike fixed dinner. At the end of the evening they went to bed alone. Blue tried to find large unappealing t-shirts and sweats to walk around the house in. They tried not to be sexy at all for each other. That was a complete disaster because Mike seeing Blue in any way or in anything turned him on. The fact that she tried to make herself unappealing was sexy to him. He loved her and everything about her. Thanksgiving morning was upon them. Phone calls and texts came in and went out with cute little sayings and pictures of turkeys.

Social media was full of memes about Thanksgiving. The news showed the president pardoned a turkey, but chickens were being sacrificed all over the White House. Coco sent her a picture of her belly with the caption, *"No need for me to have turkey today, I already swallowed one."* Blue almost dropped her phone she laughed so hard after reading it. She took a picture of her belly and sent back *"me too."* Mike looked at her. He couldn't figure out what was so funny. She showed Mike the pictures of the bellies and the captions. He shook his head and chuckled. He asked Blue to call Ms. Deb and see if it were too late to bring anything. She instructed them to bring themselves and that would be all they needed. She reminded them that dinner was at three o'clock and she couldn't wait to see them.

He stepped out of the shower and stopped. He looked at her and smiled with a heart of thanksgiving as he stood in the bathroom door and watched her. It still didn't seem real. He couldn't believe that after all this time, the woman he loved most was in his house, in his space and reciprocating his love.

"What?"

"Nothing just wanted to take in my beautiful pregnant future wife and give a shout out to God Almighty for answering prayers."

Blue's heart melted. She imagined jumping on him ripping his clothes off and riding him long and strong, but she remembered what the pastor said. So she just rubbed her belly, swallowed hard and walked away in a look of defeat.

"What is wrong with you now?" he looks at her confused.

"I need to repent because I just had great sex with you in my mind!"

"Girl you so crazy!"

Mike looked at her, blushed a little and gave a side smirk. He felt a type of way being left out of great sex with the one he loved.

"Dang, now I know how you felt," he shrugged.

"I wonder if yours was as good in your mind as it was in mine!"

"Well if it were anything like making love to you in the flesh, I would like to go smoke a cigarette and come back for round two."

They both bust out laughing.

"Go get your butt in the shower silly. I will make us breakfast."

Blue waddled off to the bathroom and Mike threw on some shorts and started breakfast. They both burst out into laughter again. She got out of the shower, threw on some clothes and sat at the table. She was greeted with a thin waffle, bacon, an omelet and cut up some pieces of fruit. He sat her orange juice on the table.

"Mike this is a lot of food. We are going to Ms. Debs in a few hours. I can't eat all of this."

"Blue why are you lying," he laughs. "Believe it or not your appetite has picked up. You know in thirty minutes you will look at me and tell me you are hungry. By twelve o'clock. Guarantee it! You can eat what you want babe and be done. If you eat it all I won't tell. Just feed my boy!"

"You are back-to-back with the jokes of the day Mr. Long." she whimpers. "Leave me alone Mike you know I am sensitive."

"Okay I'm sorry," he said as he kissed her on the forehead. "Now eat your breakfast. When we finish I have to take you somewhere and show you something."

They continued breakfast. When they finish she cleaned the kitchen, and they left the house. They arrived on the outskirts of downtown at this big building. Mike parked and they looked around then went inside. She could not believe her eyes. This place had all kinds of family fun and entertainment. There was a stage to showcase local young singers, poets, and bands. Along the wall was an area to hang the art of the up-and-coming artists. It had small rides and games. There was a food bar that would sell individual and family style items. Big televisions mounted the walls in one room for sporting events.

They walked out back to the batting cage and baseball field where little league teams would come to play championship games. The concrete poured and some of the brick wall had been autographed by legendary baseball players. The space brought Blue to tears. She was so overcome with the place she had to sit down for a second. It seemed too good to be true. She was thinking this had to be a dream because she had never heard of love like this in real life. In movies sure, but not up close and personal. The closest she had seen was Delmar and Celeste but to experience it for herself was something that she only wished as she prayed for it. The love he so freely showed was incredible.

"You ok?"

"Yea baby I am. I was just taken aback by all of this. When did you even have time to do this?"

"I have always had this in the plans for my first-born son. Had he been a girl I would have started on the space I have for her. If we have another boy I have a business plan to handle that as well. And the profits that are made off these businesses will go into a trust fund for them. Any money banked is theirs. I don't foresee us needing it. They can have it once they turn twenty-one or twenty-five depending on their maturity level. I want us to teach them how to be good stewards over their allowance and birthday money so when they get the large sum they won't go a fool. They won't be out trying to blow it on everything and have nothing to show for it. Matter of fact they won't know anything about this until they are of legal age."

She could not believe her ears. She wanted to slap herself hard! It amazed her that even as his best friend, she was never privy to any of this information. Mike was very strategic in how he handled his business affairs. She got herself together and grabbed him tight. She knew the relationship would have moments where it may have its difficulties, but she promised herself she would work at being a good wife and mother. She owed that to her husband and children. They rode by big Mike's and went inside for a while.

She remembered when he began to make this dream a reality. He told her that it would happen, and it did. Mike had an awesome business head, and in less than a year and a half later this man has the number one spot in the city. He was also getting ready to open a new business under the name of his son. She sat at one of the tables while he checked on the lounge. He believed people that had families should be off so his place of business would not be open on major holidays. The lounge was open Monday through Wednesday during brunch and dinner. Thursday night through Saturday night as a lounge. At any given time, a live artist may be in the lounge on Friday night. Saturday he used for amateur night and live bands. People loved the spot and the feel it had to it.

People liked coming to sit on the couches and love seats and watching the flat screen televisions and on cold nights hanging out by the multiple fireplaces and watching the long fish tank in one of the walls. There was a night dedicated to jazz and old school music. Once a month he had a hip-hop night. Mike loved music and he was a big jazz and easy listening kind of guy. That is one of the things the people loved about his spot. You could also go upstairs and have dinner on an open balcony. Every first and third Sunday was gospel night. He had live gospel artist come in and have praise and worship. There was something for everyone interested. He signed a contract and left it in the office on the desk. Blue had not been in there in a while. He showed all the finished upgrades. As they talked, he rubbed her shoulders and kissed her forehead.

"I feel like I have not been here in forever. This place really looks good babe."

"Thank you beautiful. You know I try," he said. "I have started something, now I have to continue to keep it fresh and inventive."

"Yes you do. You and your staff have done an amazing job with this place."

"Praise God," he said. "Well beautiful are you ready to head over to Ms. Deb's? I am sure she won't mind us being early?"

"Yea. We can start that way. Can we stop first and get me a snack? I am hungry."

He laughed as he wished he would have bet her about being hungry. They leave and stop off at a little restaurant. He ordered her a salad. She ate it on the ride to Ms. Deb's. They took the scenic route, so the ride took a little longer than usual. They still arrived at her house earlier than the other guest. Jenna stood and waited for them on the porch as they parked the car. The kids met Mike and Blue on the sidewalk and greet them with handshakes and kisses. They all went inside. Mike and Blue continued with the greetings. Blue kicks her shoes off and ask Ms. Deb if she wanted any help. Ms. Deb kindly pointed to a few items in the kitchen that could use Blue's attention while instructing Mike to sit and watch the game with Mr. Jim. Blue enjoyed helping in the kitchen. She thought about how their house would be during the holidays as the boys ran in and out. Jenna came into the kitchen with the ladies and talked to Blue for a while.

She found it pretty interesting that a human life formed inside of another human body. She was too young to remember her mom being pregnant with her brothers. Jenna asked the ladies a few questions about sex and childbirth. She noticed baby Kristopher moving. She spent a few minutes getting acquainted, her phone rang and playtime with baby Kristopher was over. It was three o'clock and guests began to arrive. As everyone came in they did the standard greetings. After about thirty minutes it was time to eat. Mr. Jim blessed the food and encouraged the family to give Ms. Deb a round of applause for her great efforts in the kitchen. While their family made a fuss over how great the food looked, Ms. Deb made plates. She was hungry and ready to eat the meal she stood in the kitchen and prepared over the course of the week. Everyone followed suit. She was thankful that she could provide a delicious dinner for her family and friends to enjoy. After some having second and third helpings they laid around for a while.

A short time later they played games. It was the younger generation against the older and women against men. They had a ball yelling and shouting answers all evening. Before they knew it midnight was upon them. The guests said their goodbyes and left for their perspective homes. Mike and Blue were the last two to leave. Blue kept Ms. Deb company while she put what was left of the the food in the fridge. She put the dishes in the dishwasher and walked Blue and Mike to the door. They kissed the sleeping children balled up in a strategic knot together on the couch and said their good nights to Ms. Deb and Mr. Jim. As they rode home they replayed the fun they had that evening. They go in the house and get ready for the morning. They kissed each other good night and went into their separate corners of the house.

Morning came and Mike drove Blue to work. Although she would never admit it, Blue quickly grew accustomed and liked the routine of being chauffeured to work by her love. The work hours seemed to move at snail's pace. The office was only opened until noon, but it took forever to come. Mike patiently drove Blue around after work to run errands. She had plenty to run since Coco's baby shower was the next day. He didn't really mind because he enjoyed her company. If she was happy, he was happy. She picked up gifts and other things needed for the baby shower. Baby Grace Camille's colors were pink and chocolate with a hint of mint green. She lucked up and found those colors in everything she needed from the party supply store. She ordered balloons and found games for both the women and men to play. She left the store with a trunk full of goodies.

Since Mike had been such a great sport about the errands and looking after her, she treated him to dinner at a quaint little restaurant across town from her old home. Even though they had a housekeeper come in two days a week, Mike was still hands on with the running of the house. When Blue tried to help he pitched a fit. He made it very clear that while she carried this baby, she in his mind was high risk and wanted not so much as laundry to be a stress factor until after she gave birth. She could not lift a finger. He toyed with the idea of bringing the housekeeper in a few more days a week now that he was also the bodyguard.

He also told Blue to start looking for a part time nanny. Although he worked nights he had business to handle during the day the baby needed to be in the comforts of his home. Between the women and Jenna with their planned stays Blue would have more than enough help for a little while. It would be when she went back to work that Mike would need help with the baby. He knew Blue saw him as her superhero but realistically he also knew he couldn't do it all and in order to continue to be her superman and give her the good wood as often as he planned he knew he would need help. This transition would need all hands-on deck.

They go inside and have dinner. The restaurant was much like the one he liked in his hometown. It was Mike's first time eating there and the experience was enjoyable. There wasn't much talking over dinner. They were swimming in ribs and fried fish, collards, potato salad, macaroni and cheese with an inch-thick piece of cornbread. They washed it down with a glass of sweet tea. Too full to speak, Mike grunted for the waitress, paid the bill, and left. They shared a love for the songs Mike had on the playlist in the car. He put his hand on her leg and she rested her hand on his and they rode home with only the noise of the radio. She moved her hand up to his neck and rubbed the back of his head.

He exhaled as he enjoyed the movement of her hand running back and forth over his neck. He could fall asleep to her touch. It was soothing, refreshing, purifying. They made it home. She sent Mike to his room to lay down before work. He promised he wasn't going to be out long. He knew he had to prepare food for the baby shower the next morning much. She thanked him for being such a support. To show her appreciation to him she booked him a needed and deserved massage. She promised after he brought the food in, he could skip out and have some downtime. She didn't want him to feel pressured to be under her all the time. She encouraged him to have this time to himself. She told him the time and address of his appointment. He hesitantly agreed, thanked her with a kiss and took a short nap. Mike's alarm went off. He laid there a minute and collected his thoughts. He showered and dressed. On his way out he walked in Blue's room.

She wasn't there. He found her wrapped in a blanket on the couch watching television. He asked was everything ok sitting down beside her. She leaned her head on his chest telling him she couldn't sleep. He said a prayer over her and encouraged her to lay down and get some rest. His touch made everything better. He had never been to a baby shower but from the preparation he saw, he knew her day would be full. He held her for a few minutes longer and watched her movie with her until the commercial break. He kissed her gently on the forehead and tells her goodnight. He closed the door and she set the code for the alarm. She cut off the lights and television and crept her way to her bed. Just when she fell off to sleep she heard footsteps in the house. She grabbed her bat and moved quietly beside the wall. Mike walked in her room to check on her. She hit him with the bat.

He grabbed the bat from her and made himself known. He was glad he had the gun put up in his room and hadn't given her access to it yet. She did well at the practice rang so splattering him against the wall would not have been an issue. She grabbed him an ice pack for his shoulder and apologized repeatedly. She felt horrible that she did it, him but she showed him she could take care of herself.

"Mike, honey I'm sorry! I wasn't expecting you."

"Well I am here now. Oh how about your boy was in the lounge tonight when I got there."

"Oh my God. What happened?"

"Not a thing. He looked at me and I looked at him. He knew better. I won't discriminate against money. Since he knew how to behave himself I was cool. He knows that is my spot but hey. Besides, he and his boys dropped twenty-five hundred in drinks and food. Buying rounds for the entire club. You know had he said or tried anything I stay strapped and ready. I guess he thought he was doing me a favor. I don't need his money but if he is giving it. I will gladly take it and when you have the hottest spot in the area, then well."

Blue was speechless. She didn't think Big was foolish enough to show up at Mike's place of business. Let alone spend twenty-five hundred dollars on a bar tab in an establishment where he hates the owner. Blue looked at Mike with fear in her eyes. Big kept showing up in the places connected to her. They agreed he must have played somewhere close to be in the city this time of year. Mike held Blue tight and assured her she was okay and Big could not get to her. She wanted to believe him and about anything else she would have. She took a deep breath and closed her eyes. When she opened them again the morning sun softly climbed through the window. She tried to get out of bed without waking him. He tried to persuade her to lay back down for a few minutes.

"Wait bae. I am going to the bathroom." she said.

He quickly let her go. She came back and laid with him a while longer. She finally got up and left him asleep. She showered and cooked breakfast. Mike woke up to the smell of pancakes with sausage and scrambled eggs. At first he thought he was dreaming. He reached over for her to find she was not in bed. He got up and followed the scent to the kitchen.

"Baby what are you doing?" he asked.

"Michael Long you are going to stop playing me about cooking. I told you I can cook. Now go sit down sir and have your breakfast."

"I am sorry. You don't cook, so I forget you can," he teased.

"Mmmmmm hmmmmmm."

They sat down to breakfast. He apologized again to her for the non-cooking remarks. She apologized about the bat and inquired about his shoulder. They ate and had small talk during breakfast. He told her of the special guest he had coming to perform and invited her to the lounge for a night out. She agreed. They cleaned up from breakfast and Mike went and laid across his bed and went back to sleep. Blue passed the window and seen an unrecognizable car sitting on the side of the road. Her heart dropped as the car door opened. She stood there paralyzed in fear. She could not move, breathe, or even call out to Mike. She feared it was Big, but she could not see his face clearly. From where she stood this person stepping out of the car looked a lot like him. She didn't hear or see Mike when he walked up behind her and called her name. She screamed turning and grabbing him, locking down on his arm.

"Big, he, he is outside baby call the police," she stammered.

Chapter 9

He sat her down on the couch, took her in his arms and begged her to calm down and breathe. He assured her it was not him. It was his friend Kevin coming to adjust the cameras for Rick since he was in the neighborhood. He promised her that Big could not get to her. She cried even harder. She felt like a fool. She was mad at herself for allowing Big to send her into hysteria. Mike offered her a glass of water. She finally settled down. He went outside and talked to Kevin. The conversation was brief. Mike came back in the house. He prepared the light hors d'oeuvres for the baby shower as she rested on the couch. He finished up and laid behind her. Together they slept until it was time for them to go to the baby shower. They arrived at Coco and Rod's in time to set up the food, games, and gifts. During their greeting Coco apologized for not being able to make Big Mama's funeral. As promised Mike left for his scheduled massage.

He left his massage and had a round of drinks with a couple of friends. Blue's transformation of Coco and Rod's home was welcomed and appreciated. She had everything they needed to welcome the guests of baby Grace Camille. The guests arrived and were greeted by the two childhood friends and their bellies. The house was full of people coming to shower Coco and Rod with love and gifts for their firstborn child. Blue gathered everyone around to play games while they ate. The games and laughter went on for a couple of hours. They cleaned up from the games and opened the baby shower gifts. For the next forty-five minutes everyone including the men oooohed and aaaaawed over the sweet little items. Coco even opened gifts mailed to them in honor of their special day. Her most special gift was the one she received from baby Kristopher. Blue thanked all the guests for coming and turned the floor over to Coco and Rod.

They again thanked everyone for coming and being blessings in their lives. After Blue passed out the keepsake boxes, many guests said their goodbyes and left. A few hung back and helped clean up. They put away the new baby items in her room. Coco was not much of a decorator, so she hired an interior designer to decorate their baby's room. The room had freshly painted pink walls and plush chocolate carpet. Elephants in all sizes danced on the accent wall behind the changing table. The ivory-colored crib was home to pink and green bedding trimmed with a dark brown border with baby Ava's name personalized in the corner.

Blue shared with Coco the décor of Kristopher's room and how her family pitched in to decorate under the direction of Celeste. They continued to talk as Blue held out her hand and introduced her old best friend to her five-caret new best friend. The ladies screamed and rejoiced at the great things that was happening in their lives. Rod ran out of the kitchen to check on them. He saw they were ok and continued to clean up. He listened to them talk and laugh all over the house. Blue filled Coco in on all of the Big drama that had taken place over the last few weeks. Coco sat on the edge of her seat with her eyes glued to Blue's mouth hanging on every word. She could not believe her friend endured so much and she wasn't able to be there for her.

She apologized to her friend for not checking in. Blue eased her mind letting her know she was fine, and everything was okay. She and Mike were moving forward as best they could and would soon be husband and wife. She went on to tell Coco in frustration that after the hospital scare Mike wouldn't let her do anything for herself. She even vented about how he is now her personal chauffeur since she thought she was being followed. She unapologetically threw in that she whacked Mike with a bat last night when she thought he was an intruder. Coco spit water everywhere when Blue mentioned Big being at Mike's lounge last night and how he'd ran up and paid a twenty-five-hundred-dollar bar tab.

She asked Blue to repeat what she clearly heard the first time. She gained her composure and tried to understand where Blue's annoyance came from but what Mike did made sense especially with everything she had already endured. Coco had absolutely no explanation for last night's event. Neither could believe he would show up at the lounge knowing it was Mike's. He didn't cause a problem being there, but the fact remained. Just then the doorbell chimed. It was Mike coming to take his little lady home. Coco greeted him with hugs, kisses, and high-fives.

"What's going on guy? Congrats on the engagement and the little man," Rod spoke up.

"Thanks man. Hey, congrats on baby girl. I hope these two were on their best behavior, especially mine. I hope they were not in here over working themselves."

"Yea they were cool. Hey man you know you could have stayed. I could have used the extra testosterone. Coed today was fifty women and two men."

"Dang son. I wanted too but my lady thought it was necessary for me to have a minute for myself. Quite frankly I am glad she persuaded me to do so. I feel like a new man."

They said their goodbyes, plan to get the ladies together for dinner before baby Ava arrived. Coco and Blue hug and she sends Blue off with a special thank you gift for all she did to make her day special. Mike and Blue left. Mike took his tired fiancé home. He promised her a bubble bath and a foot rub. He reminded her about the special guest band at the club and asked if she still wanted to go. Her mind said yes but her body could barely make it out of the car. She waddled in the house and waited on Mike to run her bath water.

She offered him to join her, but he gracefully declined. He wanted to make love to her from his soul but his promise to God replayed in his mind. She called for Mike to come quick. He ran in frantic, only to find she wanted him to watch the baby move. As he got closer he could see Kristopher stretching. He noted his little foot imprint on her stomach. Mike's eyes and smile widened. He'd seen his son move but never like that. He put his hand on her belly and felt him move. Everywhere he put his had the little fella would kick it. Mike leaned over and kissed Blue's belly. He was in aww at the baby's activity. He understood her excitement. He kissed her gently on her cheek. Seeing her naked body in its full beauty made him want her even more.

He went in his room and took a cold shower instead and met her in the living room for the massage he promised. Feeling refreshed from the bath and massage, Blue decided she did want to go to the lounge and have a little music therapy. She called Coco and Rod to join them, but Coco had been asleep since Blue and Mike left their house. They put on clothes and met each other in the hallway to show off their garments. This was the first real date they had ever been on. He helped her with her coat, and they left for the lounge. They arrive and valet parked his car. The couple was escorted to the front table of the VIP section.

There were whispers and inquiries about the owner and the pretty young lady with the glow he walked in with. Blue didn't frequent the establishment much so even some of the staff didn't know who she was. Mike informed his team that he was not there for business. He was a guest having a great time with the love of his life. The music was terrific, the food was superb, and the ambiance was heavenly. Mike took his lady by the hand and danced with her for several songs. When she'd had enough they sat back down and continued to listen to the live performance.

During the band's break, he called over the drummer and introduced the group to Blue. They took a few pictures, signed some autographs, and continued their set. In her mind, Blue planned to hang until last call, but she couldn't make it past eleven thirty. It was the best two hours of her life. Mike looked at her and smiled as she tried to fight the sleep that was about to take over and win. He called for his check, paid the tab, and took his sweet amor home. By the time they were down the street she was asleep. Mike woke her with a kiss and helped her inside the house. On the way to her room they briefly talked about which church service they would attend the next morning.

"Did you have a good time love?" he asked.

"The best. Although all times are good with you." she winked. "Hey which service shall we attend in the morning?"

"Eleven is fine. I may need to pay admission since we haven't been in so long," he said.

"I know right. They might make us feel out visitor or new members cards," she joked.

"Dang, has it been that long?" he said confused.

"It has been about a month for you. I went last week," she teased.

He pulled her shoes off and helped her out of her clothes. She slipped on her pajamas and crawled into bed.

"Bae! You're going to be a mommy," he gleamed.

"I know, and you-a daddy. What do you think about that?"

"Well I never really thought about it until right now. I mean yeah, I know he is in there. Even playing with him there is something a little different Kris. I can't explain it. Don't get me wrong it is a feeling I like."

"Baby I know exactly what you mean. I have the same feeling. Soon he is going to be here with us."

They were officially about to be parents. They only had four more months of it just being the two of them. They were excited and a little nervous at the same time. Sure between them they had a niece and nephew, a couple of godchildren that they prayed nothing ever happened to their parents and three very special children that adored them but that was nothing in comparison to bringing their own bundle of joy home to care for. Yea she had an abundance of patients, but she never had to see them past well visits and yearly physical exams. She reached out for Mike's hand. He knelt down beside her and they prayed. Mike ended prayer asking favor and protection over their family and friends and for God's covering over his future wife and child. They both get in the bed. She tucks her body into his as tight as she could and held on to him for dear life. He kissed her and rubbed her face gently as she dozed off. He held on to her all night until morning came and found them in the same position. The alarm clock sounded as a reminder that rest time was over and it was time to start the day. Mike hit the snooze a couple of times. He didn't want to let her go. He wished for an online church service so he could keep her close to him. She felt so good in his arms. He greeted her with a morning kiss. Blue went to shower. Drying off, she saw Mike standing in the door with his camera.

"Michael Long, what the ham are you doing?"

"I want to capture you in still life. You being pregnant is just too beautiful not to have on film. So cover up your personal parts and I will take pictures of you guys."

Blue did as she was requested. They took several pictures of her in the bathtub. He took a few on the bed and couch of her in her robe. He gave her the camera. She took pictures looking down at him touching, kissing, talking, and playing with her belly. They found their way into the bedroom in front of the long, gorgeous mirror. She took pictures of their reflection. They took a few more. They finished taking pictures and decided on a few they would put in his nursery and in the hallway. She dressed and bundled up, grabbing a snack on the way out the door. The mini photo session almost had them late for church. The drive seemed longer than usual. Blue looked over at Mike occasionally.

"What bae? What is it?" he asked.

"Nothing."

Blue looked at him and her eyes filled with tears. She could only muster the words thank you as her heart leaped for joy in her new happiness. She put her hand on his leg and rubbed his thigh. It amazed her how he loved her with no rules, no walls, and no contingencies.

"For what beautiful?"

"For loving me and my…. I mean our unborn child. Thank you for the way you handle me and make a fuss over our well-being. For the way you make me feel special. The way you have shown me how real love from a real man is supposed to look and feel like. Loving me unconditionally as a best friend for the past eight years and now as my lover and fiancé. The way you love me as a future husband and father of our children. For not being afraid of my success. But for being the beautiful soul you are. I wish I saw you eight years ago through the eyes I see you through now."

"I told you if you let me I would be all in. I try to make good on my word. I meant everything I said to you Kris. I've loved you for a long time and I promised God that if I ever got the chance   I would not give any lip service about making you happy. I would listen to your heart and love you. Besides, the dynamics of our relationship would not be the same as it is now. See we both had to go through some things in order to appreciate where we are. Sure we haven't started this relationship like a normal couple, but our relationship is ours and all that does or doesn't come with it."

She leaned over and kissed his cheek moving her hand close to his man part. Startled he swerved the car a little.

"Girl, I cannot be explaining to anybody why my business is up and visible on my way into the house of the Lord," he shrieked.

"I am so sorry, my hand slipped when I leaned in," she giggled.

As they neared the church they noticed the parking lot was a little fuller than usual. They figured it was visiting family and friends that had not gone home from the Thanksgiving holiday. They parked and went inside. The church was packed. Lucky for them, Ms. Deb and the family saved them a seat on their pew. Pastor Williams delivered a soul stirring message entitled *The Enemy Within*. A message that persuaded one to get out of the world and get in God's will. After church Jenna and the boys begged to go home with Blue and Mike since they had hardly spent any time with them lately. Mr. Jim hurriedly agreed. He pointed out that it would give them some alone time as well and it would be nice to be with her and have no distractions. It would be a win for all.

"Jim, baby what about all of the food I cooked for Sunday dinner?"

"Well darling we will just have to eat it for Monday dinner. Nothing wrong with that."

"Well yeah that will be fine," she agreed.

"While the kids are gone you and I can do dinner and a movie. It has been quite some time since I have been able to have your undivided attention. I would like to give you some extra attention."

"Well honey I would love that. Mmmm especially the extra attention," she blushed. Ms. Deb reminded the kids to be good. They agreed on a Sunday afternoon date. The kids piled in Mike's jeep and they cut up the whole way. They stopped by the store and picked up junk food. They turned on the road close to the house when Blue saw she had a missed message from Rod. He was calling to let them know that Baby Grace Camille had made her debut into the world. Blue told Mike of the news. Without question, Mike turned the jeep around and made his way to the hospital. They arrived and found Coco's room. The five of them piled in the room with the rest of the family to welcome the new baby. Blue washed her hands and carefully took her sweet godchild in her arms. While she was there, she went ahead and looked her over. Blue looked at the proud parents and described the beautiful baby girl as perfect. The baby started to make a fuss and Blue handed her back to her mother.

Blue facetimed Celeste and she spoke with Coco for a few moments wishing her and Rod congratulations. Blue's breakfast snack had long worn off. She was ready to eat. She kissed her best friend and Rod goodbye. She nestled her nose down in the neck of baby Grace. Mike rounded up the kids and they left. Once they were closer to the house, Mike let Jenna drive. He gave her a few pointers from the back seat with the boys. Blue closed her eyes. She didn't want to see her death coming if that were the end of her. Jenna safely parked the car and Blue sent a thank you to heaven after she put her foot on the ground. The kids ran in the house. Mike envisioned for a brief moment what life would be like with their children running around the house. Between cooking dinner Mike played video games with the boys.

Jenna and Blue painted their nails, talked about boys and her new school year. Soon the food was ready, and they met around the dinner table. There was no talking just the sound of their dinnerware clinking the plates. The boys even had a second helping. Shortly after dinner they enjoyed their snacks and a movie. They sat on the couch dinner and snack wasted. Night tiptoed upon them. The doorbell rang. Mr. Jim and Ms. Deb came to collect their dependents. The deal was to run in and get the kids, but they stood and talked for a while.

The kids told their parents all about their afternoon and how Mike let Jenna drive. They made plans to come and visit every other Sunday. Mr. Jim asked had the kids been any trouble and Mike assured him they had and teased how they ate him out of house and home. The kids continued to play the game while the adults talked. Mike told Ms. Deb of Jenna's job offers and whenever she was ready she could have her pick.

"Look at you squirt! Two job offers and not a credential to show for either one of them. Go head daddy's baby!" he laughed. "Well it is getting late and these little folks have to get ready for school tomorrow and I would like to get back to date night with my wife," he said as he winked at Mike.

"Boooooy! Mr. Jim I can't wait to have date night with the future Mrs. Long. I want to have date night alllllllllll night long. You've seen her. Whew."

Blue nudges Mike with her elbow. "Michael!"

"What!? I am just being honest."

"Hang in there young man. Count down to the days until you will be married and then you can have all the date night you can stand. Especially if she is up to it. Imma tell you man. When the Mrs. and I were dating date night was nowhere near an option. That was the longest year of my life. I couldn't even smell it. Will she at least let you smell it Mike?"

"All of us have school and work tomorrow. Say good night and let's go!" Ms. Deb interrupts as she nudges him with her elbow.

"What? Mike knows I am being honest. Even if he could smell it, if they have had one of their counseling sessions with Pastor Williams, IT'S OVER!"

"Mr. Jim you know exactly what time it is sir. My boys are on the last shade of blue-almost purple!" Mike declares. "My God!"

They laugh. Blue and Ms. Deb shake their heads at the guys. They all said their goodbyes and Mike watched them until they drove off. He shut the door. He sat up with Blue a few more minutes then went to his room to change clothes. He needed to make an appearance at the lounge. Blue looked around and noted the chores that needed to be done. She was in the middle of taking a basket of clothes to her room when Mike saw her.

"Kris! What are you doing? Why do you have that basket? I would have done that. Come on now," he bloats taking the basket in the room.

"Mike I can carry the basket. I can do things for myself baby. I am not helpless. I can live a normal life. I love you but you have got to let me do somethings too. LOOK AT ME!"

Tears filled his eyes, "I know you are ok. I know you are a fighter, and you are making a full recovery. You did not see what I saw when the ambulance picked you up. How you were laying there damn near lifeless in that hospital bed heavily sedated with that oxygen mask and I.V. connected to you. Then seeing another monitor hooked to you for our son. I thought I was losing you. I know you are a big girl and can handle yourself, but I just want to make life as stress free as I can for you baby. I just don't know what I would do if something happened to you. I don't think I could handle that."

He walked into the bathroom to calm down and get himself together. She gave him space and time to do so, but she stood outside the door. When he opened the door she greeted him with open arms.

"Baby I am fine. I know you are worried, but I am ok. I love that you want to protect me and do everything for me. I think it's hot and kinda turns me on. You have a beautiful, let me take care of it, kind of spirit. I love that. But you can relax now and let me pull more of my weight in this relationship. I don't want you to burn yourself out. Baby I got this too. I tell you what. Any time I can't do it or need help I promise to let you know. Besides, you need to rest up because when this little boy gets here, he is going to be all yours," she joked.

He held her close with the image of those three days playing fresh in his mind. He wasn't trying to be controlling on purpose. It also brought back the fear of when he almost lost his mom and how helpless she was during her recovery. He knew she was a big girl. It seemed difficult to put that part of them in the past so soon. He also knew that the same fool that put her in the hospital the first time would not let go. He has proved that he wanted to hurt her at any cost. Blue also reassured him that Big was mind over matter and that she would no longer allow him to matter to the point that it would alter her state of wellbeing like he did before. He figured he would take her word for it and start letting her drive herself to work at least a few days a week. They felt the baby kick. Blue looked down and rubbed her belly.

"See daddy we know how to get people off of us when we need too."

He pulled himself together and went to the lounge. Blue put away her clothes then put herself to bed. The next few weeks went by very quickly and life was better than good for them. Work was busy and booming. Blue's doctor visits were going great and baby Kristopher grew as he should. The meetings with pastor Williams were enlightening and informative. She and Mike were happier in love and there was no sign of the real baby's daddy. Every morning she called her mother on the way to work or on the way home. Her mom kept the conversations short. She didn't want to be the one to ruin the surprise. All of the secret keeping was stressful. Blue almost suspected something when Celeste showed up and spent the weekend with them and having what she called a pre-celebratory outing. It was mid-December and cold.

Celeste almost had to order in. Blue was not one for winter weather. She put on the thickest sweater and tights she could find and wrapped up in her heavy coat and braved the night. They reminisced about their childhood and how Big Mama would be so proud of her. They shared many laughs and an abundance of tears. It was a weekend that would never be forgotten. Finally the week everyone had been waiting for had finally arrived. It was the week they counted down to Christmas Eve. Everyone had their marching orders for the ceremony. Celeste made Ms. Deb's home for the week. Rod brought the kids a few days before, his mom came and helped. While Blue was at work, she stopped by the house and grabbed the rings and Blue's dress. The day finally arrived. Mike and Blue could finally become one. Christmas Eve morning Mike and Blue got up as usual. In Blue's mind they were just having dinner like they planned at the lounge.

She had no idea it was her wedding day. She knew the day was coming but she figured they would get up and go to the justice of the peace. She even thought about having Pastor Williams come to the house and perform a simple wedding ceremony amongst the people she loved most. While Blue showered and dressed, Mike moved like a secret agent as he hurriedly packed the car trying not to be caught. On the ride to the lounge Blue gleamed with excitement about the anticipation of the day. When they arrived at the venue, she noticed a stretched limo close by.

She pondered in her mind who could it be for. She asked Mike was anyone special coming to dinner she didn't know about. He winked and replied just her. She smiled and put her hand on his face and kissed him. He helped his lady out of the car and escorted her to the door in the fresh dust of snow. He opened the door, and they were greeted by cheers, and voices yelling surprise from all over the room. Blue was beyond shocked. She could not believe what she saw. She hugged and greeted her family and friends noticing they were in formal attire. Celeste and Coco ushered Blue to the assigned dressing area. Blue put on her dress and Celeste did her makeup. Mike put on his suit and readied himself for this day he'd patiently waited eight years for. Mama Bella gathered herself and walked her baby girl down the aisle. The transformation of the lounge was breathtaking.

Big floral pillars in the space created an aisle for her to walk down accompanied by a full orchestra playing. Sheer chiffon and voile fabric draped from the ceiling with lights intwined. The tables were adorned with blue sequin tablecloths accented with different sized three-dimensional mirror pieces and tall glass vases. There were multiple arrangements of beautiful feathers flowing from the top with an assortment of silver candle holders that held lit flames. Little miss Makenzie threw flowers, then stood beside her mom. Blue walked until she met her love at the front of the room. Mike surprised her with a small wedding party. Pastor Williams smiled at her as if he gave the last of his seal of approval. At the front stood her sister Celeste and childhood friend Monica. Jenna along with Mike's goddaughter held the title of bride's maid.

She met him standing in front of a floral wall with flowers of different sizes. Standing with Mike was Mr. Long. Don stood in as his other best man. Chuck and Delmar stood as his groomsmen. Delmar Jr stood handsomely in his tuxedo with his pillow for the rings. She could not believe this day was here and finally happening. Mama Bella kissed Blue and Mike. She went to her seat when directed. Pastor Williams continued the ceremony and then turned the floor over to Mike and Blue. They exchanged their expressions of love in the way that they chose to each other.

Mike cleared his throat and began, "Kris, I promise to love you and be there for you. I promise to be fair and do my part as your husband and as the head of our house. I promise to seek Godly counsel if and when it is needed for us to get through the tough times. I can't promise there will not be any, but I can promise, as God allows, I will always be there to help see you through them. I promise to support you in your dreams and goals. I promise to listen and be respectful. To always be honest and loving. I promise to never be too busy for us and our family. I vow to share my hopes and dreams with you. I promise to love our children," he reached over and put his hand on her stomach. "Today my love we are officially one. You are my best friend. You are my love and my everything. I vow to love you every day with all I have and all I am. Our souls were destined to connect. You were molded from my rib and the best part of my heart. We will walk together. I shall never walk ahead of you or ever leave you to walk this road behind me or alone. I pray God gives me a renewed strength to love you daily more and more if that is at all possible."

Blue allowed the tears to flow freely from her eyes. The families whistled and cheered. Mr. Long yelled out, "my boy!" Celeste handed her a tissue, and she wiped her face. She smiled at Mike. She took a deep breath and through the sniffles she began.

"Mike today, tomorrow and forever. I am yours. To have-to hold-to mold. I was made from the best of you, so I generously give it back. I give you the best of my love and my life. The best of me as a mother and wife. We have grown past friends to lovers and back to friends again. My heart is yours to adore. I give myself to you as I have never to another. We enter this Holy and Sacred covenant of marriage with God knowing I was created for you as your blessing. You found me, your favor, your never-ending good thing, crafted by God Himself just for you. Your gift to open and explore. As we journey this life together, I promise to be a listening ear and a sounding board. I will walk beside you and never in front of you. I promise to follow you as you follow Christ. I promise to always protect and remember our love. It is why we are standing in this moment. I will always be your number one fan and cheerleader. I devote my life to you, as a helpmate supporting you as you support and cover us. I vow to inspire you and encourage you in each new day."

The families cheered and applauded again. Tissues were passed around. Their families knew their stories and their journey. To see it all come together was a celebration indeed. There didn't seem to be a person in the building who wasn't rooting for them and their marriage to work. They settled down and pastor Williams continued. Blue handed her flowers to Monica. Celeste and Don gave their rings to the pastor. He held them up and informed the audience of the symbolism of them. He prayed over them and handed them to the couple for the ring exchange. He said one last prayer and Celeste surprised them with a vocal selection.

"And what God had joined together, let no man asunder. Family and friends I have the honor to introduce to you Mr. and Mrs. Michael Long. Mike son you may now kiss your bride." he ended.

Mike stepped forward and kissed his wife. He almost forgot they were in the presence of family and friends. Pastor Williams cleared his throat and smiled awkwardly. When they came up for air, the guests cheered and greeted them with hugs and congratulations. The couple celebrated the joining of their marriage. The families and friends enjoyed cocktail hour while the wedding party took pictures.

Chapter 10

They danced their first dance lost in the presence of each other. Celeste and Coco gave their words of encouragement as the maid and matron of honor. Don followed behind them. Mr. Long brought up the rear. He spoke to Mike as only a father who had raised and nurtured a man child could. Trying to hold back his tears Mr. Long assured Mike that he and his mother were heavenly proud of him and honored to be his parents. He thanked Blue for making his son so happy. He embraced the couple and took his seat beside his wife.

Mike and Blue walked the room greeting each of their guests. They finished and cut their cake posing for more pictures. The women eagerly rushed the floor for the throwing of the bouquet. One of the younger girls caught it. Her dad took it from her and handed it off to the closest woman he saw. As with every wedding the men had to be reminded they were single. They slowly moved, pushing each other out in front. Mike tossed the garter belt and the guys watched it fall to the floor. Someone finally reached to pick it up and hurried off the floor. The DJ invited the guest to dance. Soon this part of the day was over. Mike thanked everyone on behalf of him and Blue for coming and supporting them. They hugged their parents. Blue hugged her sister. The door was opened on the limo she inquired about earlier. Mike helped his wife through the-inch-high snow and into the car. He gave the chauffeur instructions to drive.

"Mike baby, where are we going? Are we headed for the airport? Did you get clearance for me to fly? Where are my clothes and all of my personal items? How did you pull all of this off?" she inquired with desperation.

"Girl BREATHE! I got this. It is a surprise. You will see when we get there. Sure I did. That was the determining factor of our destination. Celeste took care of all of that. Matter of fact, I owe her big. She has been back and forth helping me these past three weeks. Trying to pull this off without you knowing was hard and also why I had been extra tired lately. Our families are going to get everything back to the house. My folks are responsible for getting all our gifts and my jeep back home. We already have the kids' Christmas stuff wrapped and ready for them. We even found the stuff you bought and wrapped it too. We were moving while you were at work. Even Ramona helped. When she did your laundry I had her tell Celeste your sizes so she could get you new clothes and swimsuits. They all have an additional very nice present from us in the house waiting for them courtesy of Ramona as well. They are all spending Christmas at our house. When they are ready they know how to lock up and let themselves out. Did I do good?"

"No Mike you didn't. You my friend did phenomenal. I am speechless."

"Good. All I needed was a chance. Thank you for taking a chance on me."

"No Mike. I should be thanking you."

Still in their wedding garments, they arrived at the airport and checked their bags. They passed security and board their plane. Mike hands Blue her fully charged tablet and phone. They listen to the stewardess give the departure and landing safety precautions. She cheered quietly in her seat when she heard the pilot announce their travel destination. Mike mimicked her and they laughed. The plane took to the air. Mike let his chair back and Blue watched her movie. Tired from the prior weeks, Mike laid his head back and in no time was asleep. Three and a half hours later the pilot began giving instruction to return seats and drink trays back to original position as they prepared to land. In the sunset Blue could vaguely see the waters below the plane but she knew it was there. The lighting of the runway greeted the passengers to the beautiful island. The plane landed and they shuttled about four miles to a secluded resort.

Each living quarter had its own private entrance and excluded balcony. Mike pretended to pick up Blue and carry her over the entry way of their living quarters. They would spend the next several days venturing and exploring the island. Blue looked around the room. She looked down through a portion of the glass floor. She saw fish swim under them. She walked outside on their balcony. In appreciation she looked towards heaven and thanked God for her life. Mike walked up behind her and began to kiss her neck and shoulders. He was happy she loved the room and all, but he had an emergency that needed quick attention. He gently undressed her. He stepped back and beheld the beauty of his bride in her full pregnancy and marital glow. They showered and had small talk in the bathroom. They dried off and he walked her to the bed. Taking his time, he delighted in exploring her body. It was the anticipated moment they both had been waiting for.

They were able to freely explore each other sexually as husband and wife. He kissed her belly and talked to the baby for a minute. He began to please Blue in the way he'd never pleased another. It was his first encounter, but he quickly learned how to make her body respond to his actions. She clawed the sheets and gasped for air as he licked and sucked on the part of her that gave him the creamy goodness he was pleasuring her for. She thought to herself he could give a class and people would pay good money for those lessons. She wanted to kick herself yet again. Mike was the total package inside and outside of the bedroom. She almost hated herself for waiting those eight years. However, she was grateful that now she was the recipient of all he was giving. It was hands down the best wood and tongue to ever be laid within her.

The men she dated could do one or the other. Terrance had a gift for both, but he had NOTHING on Mike. She gained her composure and as he kissed his way back up her body, she pushed him gently on his back. She kissed his neck and licked her way down his body. As she kissed him her hair tickled his chest. He grabbed a handful and softly pulled on it. She made her way to his man part. She too was a first timer in the art of oral pleasure. In her study and watching videos, she learned how to master making much of his well-endowed good stick disappear within the walls of her mouth and part of her throat. Listening to him she could tell she took good notes. She proceeded to provide vibration to help enhance the feeling. Mike found himself in a state of euphoria. He moaned and balled his toes as she went up and down on him. Before long he grabbed her head ready to release himself.

She continued to stroke him as his soldiers escaped their hideout. He was enamored by what he'd just experienced. He laid there on the bed stretched out. He wanted to curl up and suck his thumb but the man in him wouldn't let him. She gave good throat. He was mind boggled at the fact that he not only received superb fellatio from his new bride, but she handled it like a pro and on top of that she ingested some of it... he fell in love with her all over again.

"Baby, you didn't move when it came out. Did- you- swallow-it?" he asked out of curiosity.

"Yeah a little bit of it. I couldn't move, you locked down on my head. It's not like you gave me any clear sign you were ready for it to come out!"

"My bad, I thought when my body locked and I started screaming like a girl, that was all the clue you needed!"

"Now that I know! It was my first time and I only know my ques. You are my husband, so I didn't mind but give a girl better notice next time. The marriage bed is undefiled. So I am down for almost whatever!" she winked.

"Mike looked up and yelled, "YES, THANK YOU GOD I MARRIED A FREAK!"

She smacked him, "Really that is what you say out loud?"

"I'm just kidding! For real though, where is the lie?" he said as he looked at her.

"Michael Long! It could be said that I have married a freak as well."

"Well go ahead and say it. I am just waiting for little man to get out of the way for real and it is on. I will finally make love to you unrestricted. Mmmmm I can't wait!"

He positioned her for another round. She arched her back to prepare for him. He gave her deep long slow strokes and pulled her hair again. The intensity of their love making had him almost forget she was pregnant and small framed. Their breathing was heavy. The moans and whimpers heighten. Mike began to thrust deep and harder. She screamed out. He quickly pulled out and apologized kissing the arch of her back. They changed positions. She made way to straddle him. He moved but she stopped him. She began to do all of the work and he laid there and enjoyed. She moved up and down on him and when she leaned in close he grabbed on to her and providing a rhythmic combination of short, long, slow, and quick strokes he brings her to release.

She moved off and leaned over the side of the bed. He entered her from behind and led them to a climatic state of pure ecstasy. She laid beside him and nestled there in the spooning position until night fell. He ordered room service. When the food arrived, he woke her up and they ate. They explore their private balcony. Blue grabbed a blanket and sat with Mike on the chair. Blue was full and well rested ready to enjoy her husband again. She looked back at Mike as a willing participant to let him inside. Love making between them was incredible and if she wanted to get used to him and what he was working with they were going to have to break each other in. She climbed in the love seat. She dozed off and on while they basked in their love making and looked out over the water covered by the moonlit sky. The sun came up and so did Mike. He woke Blue with another round of pleasure. When they finish, he went to the suitcase and pulled out a small box and handed it to her. It was a small locket with their wedding date engraved on it.

"Merry Christmas Mrs. Michael Edward Long." he said between kisses.

"Aww, thank you baby. Wait here, I have something for you as well."

She ran to her purse and pulled out a gift for him. It was a 24-caret gold watch with *all my love forever* engraved on the back of it. They laid and held each other and looked at their wedding rings. Even though they were living it, they couldn't believe it. For a very long time he envisioned that moment. He enjoyed the beauty that was her. Many let downs and heartache led her to this place, but for her to get there she didn't mind the journey. He thanked God a million times for giving him the perfect woman. For him it was her smile that lit the room and the way her eyes danced when she was excited. He was impressed by her heart that was full of love to give to the one worthy of receiving it. Just being who she was made him want to be in her total presence. She too was thankful that she became aware of his love for her. She loved that he knew how to treat a woman and expected nothing in return although she was willing to give him everything she had. She loved his old school soul and his wisdom and understanding of things. She loved his sense of style.

Most importantly she loved him. She prayed that he stayed wrapped up in love with her because she planned to be wrapped up in love with him. Morning, noon and twice at night while on their honeymoon, Mike and Blue made love. In between the time they ate and played in the water. They had dinner on the beach by tiki and candlelight a few nights. They left the room on limited occasions to sightsee. They made as much love as they could before they had to leave the Island.

That was their main mission. There fun on the island came to an end and it was time to go but first, Mike had one more stop up his sleeve. From Aruba they spent a few days in Vegas. Neither had ever been to sin city. Over the few days they were there they took in several shows. They met the criteria of newlyweds to be in the magic show when the magician campaigned for volunteers. She surprised him with tickets to an X burlesque show one evening after dinner. Mike knew her favorite artist would be there that weekend, so he surprised Blue with concert tickets and VIP passes. She had seen them in concert several times, but she had never actually been up close and personal. She took pictures with her favorite celebrity group and had them autograph a t-shirt she bought.

They did more site seeing in Vegas than love making, but they still managed to get it in. The day came for them to finally return home. When they returned, they were greeted by the noise of the radio that Mike left on all the time. He escorted Blue across the threshold of their home as husband and wife. He came back and grabbed their bags. As they looked around their home, they noticed the family had put their gifts in one central location. Blue and Mike pick up their phones and called their families to let them know they had arrived back home safely. They thanked each of them for their love and support over the past five months. It was still somewhat early, Mike walked in the kitchen and whipped he and Blue up a quick meal. He joined his bride on the couch.

They watched a movie and ate dinner. His room was

their official bedroom. She noticed that the bedroom furniture was different and sat a little higher than it did before they left. Mike had new furniture and a set of mattresses delivered. As a man he could not allow his wife to sleep on a bed and mattresses he sexed other women in. He knew what he picked out she would like because they saw it in the store when they were running errands. They both agreed that sex was interesting with other partners. They could even agree that sex was beyond satisfying the one time it happened while they were dating. Now they experienced it on a different level.

They wanted and liked making love as husband and wife. Being married took love making to a whole new level. No constraints and being able to have your mind, body and soul connect on a different parallel was indescribable. To be able to give of yourself freely and completely without holding back was more likely to happen when both were connected to each other in a sacred bond as opposed to just being intimate with someone you date. Ramona had been over and made the bed. She had even sprayed them with the sheet spray he liked. He laid his wife down on the fresh crisp sheets. He began to kiss her body and she in return did the same.

He began to stimulate her with his hand. After she answered, he moved on to enjoy her orally. Her body shook as she in no time responded. He kissed her with a heightened passion that caused her juices to flow. He put a pillow under her back before penetration. She opened her legs to receive him. He went into her. Her walls discharged moisture. As he stroked her, he kissed her breasts and her neck. He felt her vagina mold to him and loved every minute of it as he made love to her in their home. There in their bed he liberated and eliminated her of the chains and shackles. He flooded out the memories of the hurt that came before him. Even down to the last one that planted life within her. The one she swore made her question love again. With every thrust and stroke he deposited himself into her. He filled her up to drive out the others before him. To make her body a place where the soul of his love and manhood could openly dwell. As she welcomed his body she freed him as well. She gave him the freedom to relinquish some of his control in this area. Some of the women he dated were lazy lovers and he had to put in the bulk of the work.

She freed him to make love to her in ways he knew could not happen with those women in the past. They both had only had a handful of partners, but damage was left behind. They used their love making to drive all of that out. They used it as both therapeutic and pleasurable. Blue and Mike shared in this pleasure. He enjoyed making love to her and she to him. And with each thrust, grind, and stroke they emancipated parts of each other from within each other, setting the stage for there never to be room for anyone else. She was hooked like phonics on the love he gave her, and his nose was open from the way she put it down on him. Their love making was a renewed life in its form of innocence as man and wife. After their session, Blue burrowed into Mike and slept until morning. The alarm went off and the two got up and dressed for church. Their church family was happy to see them back. Pastor Williams announced them as the newlyweds.

He told the congregation to give God praise for bringing them back to the fold safely. After church Mike and Blue were invited over to Ms. Deb's for dinner. They showed the family what few pictures they managed to take between there intimate escapades. The children couldn't understand how they were gone so long, and they didn't have many pictures. Blue and Mike looked at each other and said in one voice, "We had a lot of date night." Everything was all one shade again Mike continued. Mr. Jim got out of his chair walked across the room and high-fived Mike. Blue just dropped her head and chuckled. They continued to lay around and talk. They did tell of a few highlights in Vegas and what they did there. The time had come for Mike to take his beautiful bride home. They said their goodbyes and left. Arriving home Mike noticed a car sitting off from their yard. He pulled in the garage and they went in the house. Blue became nervous. Mike comforted her and suggested since it was late for her to go lay down and wait for him. He grabbed his gun and called the police.

He watched the car until the police arrived. They lived down a short secluded paved road. There were only two more houses down their street. Each of the houses sat two acres apart. To be sitting on that street off from their house could seem intentional. The police arrived and sent the car on its way. Mike put his gun away and went to bed. Blue was already asleep. He took her within his arms and thanked God that it was only two teenagers. He couldn't help but wonder where Big was hiding and when would he soon raise his ugly head again. She turned over and whispered, "good night." He kissed her and dozed off. They arose to the sound of the alarm clock. They arise, take showers, and leave. Mike has a business breakfast and Blue hits her eight to five.

Against his better judgement Blue encouraged Mike to let her drive herself to work. This was the whole office staff's first day back collectively. The office was closed except for the on-call nurse the week after Christmas until New Year's. She had her retired friend come in that second week, so Dr. Tomas would have help. She was back and it was business as usual. She missed seeing her patients. She and the parents had small talk about when the baby was due and how long she planned to take off with him. She assured them standard time and that Mr. Tomas would be there to continue to help her provide care for them while she was on leave. She also let them know she would always only be a phone call away and they may even see her as she had to schedule her own baby's appointments. Mike decided to surprise his wife and pick her up for lunch. When he walked in, the office staff clapped and cheered and gave him congratulatory words.

Coming from the back was one of her feisty six-year-old patients. She missed the introduction and cheers. She didn't know who he was or where he came from. She did know she liked what she saw, and she let out a loud, "mmmmm, he's cute mommy." Her mother nudged her. They laughed it off. Blue told the young lady she certainly understood why she said what she said and assured her she had those moments herself. She introduced them and the little girl apologized. They assured her there was no harm done. Mike handed her a sticker from behind the counter. She and her mother left.

"Hey lover," she greeted him. "Quite the celebrity huh?"

"Well you know how it is girl!" he smirked. "I knew you were hungry so I thought I would surprise you and take you to lunch."

"I would love that Mr. Long."

"Well then it would be my honor Mrs. Long."

The door chimed and Mr. Jim walked in. The office staff paged Ms. Deb. Mr. Jim wanted to surprise his love by coming to take her out to lunch as well. The ladies grabbed their coats and purses. Mike invited Ms. Deb and Mr. Jim to have lunch with them. They agreed and went to an upscale burger place. They were quickly seated. The waitress brought their drink order. Ms. Deb and Blue went to wash their hands. They joined their husbands back at the table.

"So how are you two enjoying married life?" Mr. Jim asked.

"Well Mr. Jim I can honestly say that these have been the best two weeks of my life. I knew it would be good, but I didn't realize how good."

"Yea, guys I would have to agree. I keep telling him I wish I had fallen for him that day we slid into our class together."

The seasoned couple laughed at the newbies and reminisced back to the time when they were two weeks into their marriage and how good things were. They apologized for laughing and ordered their meal. They offered them a word of encouragement that they promised they would need during the tough times. Ms. Deb leaned over and kissed Mr. Jim. She promised the newlyweds that she was just as much in love with her husband as she was on the day she married him. She admitted she didn't know where she would have been if

Jim hadn't rescued her. The ladies clinked their water glasses to each other for the blessing that had in their spouses. The men did the same. Mr. Jim rubbed Ms. Deb's back as they continued to talk. Mike put his hand on Blue's stomach and felt the baby move. He smiled at his wife and kissed her. The food was delivered to their table and they enjoyed their meal.

"I knew eventually you would come around. I knew from that day the very first day I was going to make you my wife. I didn't know how or when. I just knew it would come to pass," Mike confessed.

"Every time you say that I think of when my dad met my mom and in their first encounter, he told her that she would be the mother of his children. Well here sits one of them. He never got to see any of his grandkids or see his only son become a man, but oh well," she shrugged.

"Well baby I am sure he was glad he was persistent with your mom about you and your sister. I know I am. Your perfection could not have been made with any other two people."

"I am most certainly glad that you two have found each other like me and my Jimmy, right baby? I told you a long time ago when he was hanging around he was the one," Ms. Deb spoke up.

"Yes Lawd! Wise men know when they've met a good woman. It takes a fool not to love and commit to her the way God intended." Mike testified.

"Well thank you Ms. Deb and yes ma'am you did."

"Mike, on behalf of her mother and I, thank you for taking this young lady off our hands!" Ms. Deb joked.

"Ms. Deb!"

"Oh girl I am just teasing. Speaking of mama, yours walked in looking delish!"

"Yes she did," Mike and Mr. Jim agreed.

"Who was the guy she brought up with her?"

"Oh him? That was Mr. John. They have been friends for years. He hangs around and she lets him. She said he is a nice guy. He seemed to be cool every time we have been around him. She was like one marriage was enough for her. She said she enjoyed his company to the fullest though. She doesn't want to be another man's wife."

As Blue takes a sip of her water Mike chimes in, "You know he is knocking that thang down don't you?"

"Yes he is" Mr. Jim added.

Blue spit water everywhere. Their shirts and faces were full of water spots. They called for extra napkins to dry off. She apologized but in her defense, she was not prepared for the conversation she heard. She didn't want to think, let alone know anyone her mother may have even considered having sex with. Ms. Deb scolded the men for the jokes of what could have been the harsh reality of her mother. She threw her napkin at Mike.

"You don't hear me talking about your parents' sex life."

"The difference is, I am not in denial about my dad and mom having sex. The last time I rode home unexpectedly, I went in the house only to hear some unholy sounds coming from their bedroom. My dad came out of the room buck naked on his way to the kitchen. He got what he needed out of the fridge, looked at me, told me hello and went back in the room. I went to my room and cut the volume on the old stereo as loud as I could, because they clearly were not finished. My mom couldn't even look at me until the next day."

"Ok you are giving me way too much about your dad than I can take right now," she frowned.

"Mmm, try being there," he dropped his head.

Emotionally scratched, she called for the bill. Mike had the waitress put it all on one and paid it. Everyone thanked him for lunch. They finish and Mr. Jim leaves the tip. They take the ladies back to work. When they pull up to the office, they noticed Big's car in the parking lot.

"I can't believe what I am seeing. This dude refuses to go away!" she panicked.

"Ok now Mike and Blue take it easy. We are going to act like we don't see him and just maybe with us out here he will go on about his business. I will pull right up to the door and we will walk the women in and hang tight for a few minutes. Unfortunately, there is nothing you can really do. This is public property. The police won't do anything unless you say you are concerned about this unidentified vehicle sitting in your office parking lot. They may or may not check it out," Mr. Jim advised.

Mike sucked his teeth and blew, "Son of a whore!"

They all get out to go inside. He saw Blue and he revved his engine and sped out of the parking lot. They all sighed in relief. Mike made a quick phone call and arranged for his homeboy who lived in the area to ride by as he thought about it. Before Mike could tell Blue she would be chauffeured again, she cut him off and assured him it was not necessary. He did make her promise him that she would call when she left work. She agreed. The men left and the ladies went inside. As the day winded down, and she got ready to leave, Blue didn't even get nervous this time. She had already prepped herself that if Big was to come near her again she would do whatever she needed to protect herself and her child. She commended Mike for protecting her, but realistically she knew there could be a time when it may just be her and Big and she needed to be prepared for whatever went down. As they left the office for the day Blue noticed Mike's home boy outside on her way to her car. She drove towards home.

He trailed her part of the way and then he turned off. As Blue promised she called Mike and let him know she was on the way home. He didn't like the position Big was putting them in. He didn't know what he would do, but he would be damned if he lived life peeping and on edge for the next 18 years. The next morning they awake to snow. The meteorologist missed the six inches of snow that crept in on them that night while they slept. Most of the town was shut down. Mike made breakfast and Blue texted her mom and sister pictures of the fresh uninterrupted snow. They ate and Blue looked out as far as she could at the snow. Mike told Blue to get dressed. She protested and suggested they wait a while and enjoy the beautiful blanket before they made tracks disturbing it. Mike looked at her as he put on his coat and dashed outside disrupting all he could in a matter of a few minutes. He went back inside and hit her in the butt with a snowball. Pissed, Blue bundled up and waddled her way outside. She gathered snow off the banister, formed a snowball and hurled it at Mike.

They declared war and started a snowball fight. Caught off guard, Blue took a snowball to the face and fell. Mortified, Mike froze in his tracks. He ran over to her to see if she was ok. She waited on him to come close and when he kneeled beside her, she mushed him in the head with a handful of snow. Grateful she was alright, he tried to help her up. She pulled him back down in the snow with her. They decided to make snow angels. For a few minutes they had no cares in the world. They laid and played in the snow carefree- no jobs, no worries, no Big. Blue felt great and loved her life. They didn't stay out long. They came in and she warmed them some hot chocolate. They showered and snuggled on the couch. It started to snow again giving them another three inches. By nightfall, their imprints of the day were covered leaving only pictures and memories of the day.

For the next couple of days until the roads cleared Mike chauffeured Blue to work. The lounge was open for lunch, but they closed it a few hours early until the temperature was high enough that the snow stopped melting and refreezing at night. The following week an ice storm shut power down within the city for several days. Mike packed up Blue and headed south to a warmer place. They called their families to let them know they were leaving town until power and heat was restored. The power was down at the office as well, but she had all her patient calls forwarded to her. Mike and Blue spent a few days in a nice quaint bed and breakfast he found. He played music from his phone. They stood in the middle of the floor and slow danced. They never intended to make love, but it was something about being inside of her that gave them both a heighten feeling of comfort and security. It was a connectedness with a rush of adventure equivalent to free falling. It was like nothing either of them had ever experienced before and they relished in the feeling.

Chapter 11

After a few days, the power was restored. Mike and Blue returned home. In no time, Valentine's Day quickly approached. She planned a romantic get-away in the mountains for the two of them. On the drive up the mountains they stopped and took pictures. They arrived at the cabin and unloaded their things. It was already late when they got to their destination. They picked up something to eat and took it in with them. Blue and Mike showered together while listening to music. Every now and then as the Music played he would lean over and whisper the lyrics in her ear and then kiss her neck. The nibbling tickled and made her giddy. Blue decided to do something she had never done before. She turned him around. The water hits his back. She kissed down his neck and chest. She grabbed the little step stool from beside the sink and laid a towel over it.

She cautiously sat down on the stool and began to please her husband. Mike appreciated his wife. Between the hot water beating his back and his wife giving him pleasure, he didn't know whether he was going or coming. A time or two his knees buckled, and his eyes crossed. Mike released himself. Ducking his hand, she leaned back and watched his swimmers fall in the shower getting lost amongst the water and slide down the drain. He stood her up, wrapped a towel around her and walked her to the living room grabbing a blanket on the way. He laid her down in front of the fireplace he started before their shower. On the floor being air dried by the heat from the fire they made love. They laid there in their nakedness under the blanket until morning. It came quicker than they anticipated. He got up and made them breakfast. They ate and went out for the day. As they walked around they bought a few souvenirs. They bought all the kids t-shirts. The plan was to mail Makenzie and D.J. theirs when they got home. It was getting colder, so they went back to the cabin. It was Valentine's Day and Mike wanted to make Blue's favorite food. He forgot an ingredient. He ran back to town to pick it up. When he got back he found Blue curled up on the couch asleep. He rubbed her cheek and finished making dinner. Blue awakened to his gentle kisses. He helped her off the couch over to the table. They ate dinner. Still tired after dinner they curled up on the couch and in his arms she slept. They finally made their way to the bed. Before he settled in for the night he cleaned the kitchen. He joined her in bed and before long it was time to leave. They showered, dressed, and packed up. They leisurely drove home stopping at a few more shops on the way.

Between stops, Mike mentioned again about Blue owning her own gun. She was uneasy at the idea of having her own at first, but by the time they finished the three-hour drive home she was excited. She'd practiced at the range several times with his gun and she did well. He thought now would be a good time to get her her own gun to carry. She asked what the rush was. He knew he would be making provisions to travel again, and he wanted her to be accustomed to her own weapon and how to defend herself with no question or overthinking it. He wanted it to be as natural to her as breathing. He showed her a picture of her gun. She liked it. She thought it had personality. He explained to her that he had an investor/client who heard about Kristopher's and wanted to build the same type of family gaming restaurant in his town for his son. He was to give Mike a hundred and fifty thousand dollars to put a plan together. He promised it would not be like their son's, but it would be the new hot spot for families and children in that city. Blue's phone rang. Her realtor called to notify her of the closing date for her condo that sold. Blue agreed she would be there to sign her portion of the paperwork.

He knew being gone Blue would be determined to stay by herself even with the baby scheduled to come a few days before or after her due date. He planned to be back well before the baby was born but just in case he was not, he made sure she had everything she needed. He called her sister and mom and put them on standby. He asked Mr. Jim to come by and check on the house while he was away. They arrived at home and unpacked. He reminded her the grand opening for Kristopher's was in a few weeks. In one of the rooms in the back they were setting up for her baby shower. He invited Chuck and members of the team to come take pictures and autographs.

"Mike baby. What if Kristopher doesn't like baseball? What if he likes soccer or tennis or something?"

"Blue are you sleepy or did you drink some of my liquor? You are straight talking crazy! My son will like baseball because his dad likes baseball. Just that simple. My dad taught me the love and respect of the sport and I shall do the same. Besides, what is not to like about baseball?"

"Ok sir, that will definitely be all on you," she conceded.

Blue smiled with excitement about that weekend and how she loved that Mike wanted to pass something he loved down to the baby. Her eyes gleamed brightly as she listened to the events he'd planned. She casually mentioned needing a new outfit. She had no idea what she would wear. When she escorted him to the grand opening of the lounge it was grown and sexy. This is mommy and baby. She would have to search the internet to see what that looked like. By then she would be eight and a half months pregnant and miserable. Even so, she still wanted to be cute. Mike assured her that whatever she put on she would be stunning. She looked up to see them pulling in the garage. Mike put their bags in the house while Blue started dinner. She prepared them a pasta dish with fresh vegetables. Blue unpacked their bags, showered, laid in the bed, and watched television. She tossed and turned trying to get comfortable.

Mike ate, kissed his wife, and went to the lounge. He had deals to close and contracts to sign. He was feeling great about the weekend he and Blue had just shared. Baby Kristopher's establishment was coming along and on schedule. His business was flourishing. Life was better than good. He came out of the office to find Terrance and his cronies sitting at the bar. Terrance felt a different kind of stupid that night. They locked eyes. Mike tightened his jaw and walked around the bar towards the kitchen. Hyped up on steroids and drunk off hard liquor before entering the place, he had the courage to let Mike know how he felt about him and Blue. As Mike walked past Big began to make a scene. The music seemed to stop.

"Little guy running around here playing daddy to a baby that ain't his? Every time you look at her I know you know that it was the nut I busted that's growing inside her. Y'all still running around pretending to be best friends?"

"Maybe so, and for the record she's my wife now and he'll call me daddy. You can leave my place of business and you already know I will beat the breaks off you about her. AGAIN!"

"Oh, am I supposed to be scared of you boy because you got a few lucky punches?" he remarked.

"No not at all, but you will refrain from acting a fool in here, you might want to advise your boys to take you somewhere and let you dry out. You're playing a dangerous game," Mike cautioned.

The crowd began to move around the men as the argument intensified. Mike tried to keep his calm about him but Big was pushing all of the right buttons. Mike despised him for the stress and pain he put Blue through. He wanted to beat him until his soul was satisfied but he decided that would take a while. God had afforded him opportunities that built the life he'd started and could share with his wife by his side. He was trying hard not to mess that up. He didn't mind what Big said, biologically that was not his son. It was the way Big disrespected the woman that once loved him that Mike always loved that made him want to slap him to sleep. Terrance got louder and louder as the crowd grew. His boys encouraged him with laughter. Phones began to surface with fingers on the record button ready to make them internet famous as soon as the opportunity presented itself.

"This little fool right here thinks he is doing something because he married the whore that I used to let suck my nuts. Nasty tramp was really good at that!" he staggered.

"Yo, I am telling you to shut up about my wife!"

"Forget you and that nasty whore! Punk!" he punched Mike in the face. "What are you going to do?"

Terrance laughed thinking he'd gotten the up on Mike. Mike charged him and they both hit the floor. They roll and wrestle on the ground equally throwing punches. They got back up on their feet. Big put his hands around Mike's neck, Mike punched Big in the throat knocking the wind out of him. He stumbled back and before he could catch his balance, Mike kicked him in the face. Big fell to the ground unconscious. The crowd goes wild. The giant was knocked off his feet. He and his boys were escorted from the property. They were gone by the time the police arrived and Mike declared it a misunderstanding and sent the police on their way. Mike let his staff know that Terrance was not to be inside at all anymore not even to get a drink of water.

If he tried to come in again then security would escort him away from the door. He worked hard to have the number one spot in the city and even in the surrounding areas. People take the drive to come to Big Mike's and he would not let some dumb jock ruin it for him. Don checked on Mike to see if he was ok. Mike assured he was. Don prompted him to go home and get some rest. Mike grabbed a blueprint and thanked his staff. He apologized and offered complimentary drinks and appetizers to his guests. Many of them agreed they enjoyed the live action that happened. Mike promised that it would never happen again. That was not the vibe he wanted for his place of business. He got in his car and sped home waking Blue to a slamming door.

"Mike, Mike baby is that you?" she calls out nervously.

"Yeah it is me," he spoke in a rather short and distant tone.

She put her robe on and followed him in the bathroom. She noticed his eye. "Oh my God Mike! What happened are you ok?"

"Yeah I am fine. Back up off me please, just give me a second! He showed up again tonight drunk and running his mouth. Next thing I know we were fighting." he pulled away as she reached out to him.

"Oh no, I can't believe he showed up there again and this time with drama. I am sorry. Did the police come?"

"Yea but he was gone by then," he snapped.

He snatched opened the medicine drawer and slammed it back. He yelled out and hit the mirror shattering the glass. Blue looked at the man standing there that left their home as her husband. She wasn't sure who he came back as. She didn't know what had transpired in that short period of time that had him in a head space she had only heard of before. She went in the room reached in the closet and grabbed her bag and started throwing clothes in it. Mike cleaned himself up then went into the bedroom to talk to her. He grabbed her arm and she panicked and began to cry trying to pry his hand off of her. He quickly let her go.

"Baby I am sorry. I AM SORRY! I didn't mean to

snap at you. I am just frustrated as hell with this whole damn Terrance situation." he admitted.

"Do you think I am not frustrated too Mike, huh? This has not been easy for me either. I can't apologize enough for what he is putting us through. I love you and I want you happy and if you are finding that you may not be happy with me or if this is not what you signed up for, we can call this thing quits right now. Because I don't want you to spend one second unhappy especially because of me," she cried.

Mike looked at her. He grabbed her and held her tight. She fought it for a few minutes and then gave in. She knew Mike had a temper, but she had never seen it up close and personal. He persuaded her to put her bag back in the closet.

"Baby look I am sorry, and I never meant to scare you. I am not angry at you. It was him and I should have stayed out until I calmed down. I should not have brought that in our home. I'm so sorry lady love."

"Michael what happened?" she asked through the tears.

"I needed the blueprint from my office at the lounge, so I went to get it. He was in there and decided he wanted to run you down. He was being straight up ignorant and disrespectful; calling you a whore and saying you were just good for sucking his raggedy balls. I tried to keep calm until he punched me in my face, and it was on from there. We went to the ground, got up, he tried to choke me, I hit him in the throat, then knocked his butt out. No biggie. I asked him to shut up and leave but he felt he had something to prove by defaming you and trying to punk me. I remember telling you that cat was bad news. And you know he has always felt some type of way because he hated me being in the picture anyway."

Blue wiggled loose and got Mike ice for his face. Their phones chimed. They look at each other. It was his boy and a link of the video. In the text a message letting them know the video was viral. Mike put his head down. He would never hear the end of it if his mother knew about it. It didn't matter if he won. She didn't want her son tied up in that foolish and barbaric behavior. Blue kissed the place that now held a bruise from the fist of a fool. He hopped in the shower and met Blue in bed. He moved toward her, and she tightened up. He gently reached over and touched her shoulder. He apologized again to her for his conduct and how it made her feel. He kissed the back of her head and rubbed her belly. He asked God to forgive him. He asked the same of his wife.

"Can I hold you?" he whispered.

"Always," she exhaled.

She relaxed her body and he moved over and wrapped his arms tightly around her. She laid her head on his chest and rubbed his shoulder. She apologized to him for Big's hate towards him. He reminded her that Big was a grown man who made those decisions on his own. He didn't blame her for the mess big made, but he promised her that they would be okay and clean up the mess together. She kissed him. Their phones chimed a few times more. They put them on do not disturb mode.

"Baby?"

"Yea love?"

"Where were you going this time of morning?"

They both laugh.

"I don't know Mike, but I have never seen you like this ever, and it scared me."

She moved her body up against his man part as an invitation for him to find his way inside her. They engaged in their first session of makeup sex. Had she not already been pregnant she would have made this her conception date. It began to rain. As it rained outside, on the inside of the house in their bedroom tears fell like rain cleansing the negative impurities from their souls they had experienced that night. They took their time with each other making sure they both were completely satisfied. He enjoyed learning the ends and outs of her body. She took pleasure in teaching him. He replicated her touches to hers calming her body drawing her closer to him. Saturday morning thrusted itself upon them. They greeted each other in the morning sunlight. Mike cooked a light breakfast. They finished and went to the gun range. The rain continued.

The sound of it beating against the roof was calming. Mike handed her the gun and refreshed safety guidelines. She pulled the trigger on the empty gun to get used to holding it. Finally Blue was ready to handle the gun and ammo. Mike loaded the gun and handed it to her. She pulled the trigger and almost dropped the gun backing up to run. Mike caught her. She did very well her first time shooting. She didn't understand why this time fretted her so. The next couple of shots Mike stood behind her making her aware of his presence. The more comfortable she was the better she shot. Mike eased back and let her go for what she knew. After she subdued her nerves, she was killed it. They brought her target in close to see how well she did. The majority of her rounds landed center mass, neck, or head. She was very proud of herself. She continued a few more hours working up an appetite.

He informed her that her gun skills really turned him on and scared him all at the same time. To know his wife could be a lady yet handle her business when needed was beyond sexy to him. On the way home he stopped by her favorite restaurant and picked up lunch. They got home, changed out of their damp clothes, and had their meal and a movie under their blanket. In between listening to the rain they talked and laughed and had the bathroom mirror replaced. They stretched out on the pillows on the floor in front of the bay window. Before long they were making love. She wasn't making love to him to keep him. She made love to him because she enjoyed making love to him. It was just that simple.

Sunday morning rolled around. They got up and made way to the Lord's house. Ms. Deb and Mr. Jim inquired about Mike's eye. Blue did the honors of rehashing the jest of the happenings of that night. They hoped at least for now it was over, and he would honestly take the hint and leave them alone. Mr. Jim takes the gang out to dinner. Blue and Mike followed them to the restaurant. They enjoyed each other's company while they ate. Mr. Jim paid the check, and they say their goodbyes. Mike took Blue home. The next few weeks were business as usual. The time flew by and all seemed to be quiet. Blue drove herself to work with no signs of Mike's friends or

Big. She had gone to see her doctor who confirmed again she was right on schedule with the baby's due date. The baby shower and grand opening of Kristopher's was a great success.

Coco and Celeste pulled off the perfect event in her honor. People came from all over to bring their families to see the venue. There were games and prizes, pictures, and autographs. It was the perfect March afternoon. A light breeze blew, and the warm sun beamed down on them as they enjoyed the festivities of the day. Blue sat by the window and opened the gifts for baby Kristopher. When they finished, she and her friends toured the premises. She and Mike were congratulated on the remarkable business venture for the unborn son. When Blue was ready to go, they packed the jeeps with all of the gifts for baby Kristopher. Mike gave instructions to the manager and took his wife home. The house was full of baby shower guest. Everyone pitched in and helped Blue wash and organize everything for the arrival of her sweet baby boy. Mike was in the other room packing for his business trip. Blue checked behind him making sure he didn't forget anything. She kissed her love, prayed over him, and escorted him to the door. He thanked everyone for being a wonderful support and promised Blue he would call her as soon as he got to his hotel.

Blue went into her old room, picked up a bag and gave it to Celeste for the kids. Celeste complimented her on the new bed and room décor. The women sat around and continued to talk. The ones blessed to be mothers told her of their experiences. They gave her the cold hard truths about parenting but also encouraged her that it was very rewarding. Those that were blessed not to be mothers by choice reminded her of what she was giving up bringing a life into the world. Sleeping late was no longer an option they all agreed. Before they realized it, it was late. The ladies said their goodbyes and Blue set the alarm. She sat down between her mother and sister. She laid her head on her mom's shoulder and rested her hand on her sister's and basked in the blessings that was poured out on her new family. Bedtime soon approached for the women. She hugged and thanked them for their unconditional love and support. She went in her room, showered, and slept until morning. Celeste and Blue woke up to the smell of their mom's French toast. The ladies jumped out of the bed and rushed to the kitchen. The house smelled like it did when they were back in their childhood home.

Mama Bella put their plates in front of them. They finished and dressed for church. Celeste and Mama Bella loved to visit Blue's place of worship. After church they joined Ms. Deb's family at her home for Sunday dinner. They hated to eat and run but Blue had to put her mom and sister on a plane. Mama Bella decided to go back with Celeste for a few weeks to spoil the kids for a little while. They said their goodbyes and Blue thanked her big sister for always being in her corner. Celeste assured her it was her pleasure. She kissed her mother. The ladies check their bags and board their plane. Blue left the airport. She rubbed her belly and talked to her baby on the ride home. She thought to herself that she had an awesome life and then she humbly thanked God for it.

Right when she turned on her street home, her phone rang. It was Mike. He talked to her until she got in the house and locked up. He informed her that he had to stay a few extra days. Tired, she moaned in agreement. She showered and got in the bed. She called Mike back and put the phone to her stomach and Mike talked to his son. The baby responded to his voice. She hung up and she tossed and turned until she finally drifted off to sleep. She made it until morning. She got up and got to work. Work was good and she was prepared to spend another night alone. She could do it, she just had to get her head right. It hadn't been that long since she lived alone but she'd quickly gotten used to having Mike's company. She left work and noticed there was a car following her. Just like the time before when she turned the car turned. She was too far past the police station to turn around, so she just said a prayer and headed for home.

She lifted the garage and ran in the house. Scared and in a hurry, she forgot to let down the garage door. She called Mike. He was in a late meeting and missed her call. She called Mr. Jim and she could not get him on the phone either. She saw the same car that was following her outside. It wasn't a car she noticed. She thought maybe Mike sent one of his friends to check on her, but they always acknowledged themselves. She checked the camera and noticed the garage door was up. She did not see anyone. Not thinking, she ran to the side door to close the garage. She opened the door to push the button and felt a hand grab her around the throat. She coughed and gasped for air. As she dangled in the air by her neck she could not believe someone was trying to choke the life out of her with no regards for the little life growing inside of her. She knew she could not just die like that. She found the strength and began to fight. She took her nails and grabbed his face. He dropped her. She crawled across the floor trying to get away. As she crawled he followed, kicking her. She covered what she could of her stomach to protect her unborn child. She and kicked him in the groin. He fell to the floor. She got up and stumbled for the vase on the counter and busted it across his head and knocked him out. Her phone rang. It was Mike. She turned her back on him to answer the phone. Frantic, she tried to explain to Mike what happened, but it was hard to understand her through the tears. He came to and grabbed her by her hair. She screamed dropping her phone. Dragging her across the room, he picked up the phone.

"What's up turd, this pretty little whore is going to die today!" he promised.

"Let her go man you don't have to do this. Think about your career and the baby she is carrying. Don't do this man. Let her go!" Mike pleaded.

"SHUT UP! You run around town flaunting my girl and my kid. MINE!! I told her if I couldn't have her no one could. Not even you-the punk self-proclaimed best friend!"

"I swear if you hurt her I will…!" Mike began.

"You will do what? Not one thing!" he threw the phone down and focused his attention back to Blue. "Now back to you whore!"

He roared at her to stop moving. She could hear Mike yelling indistinctly through the phone. Others around him heard the commotion and asked him was everything ok. He just told him no and ran out the door. He told his business partner he had to go, and he would explain everything when he could. He jumped in his jeep and called 911. He prayed that someone would get to her before it was too late. The officers advised they were thirty minutes away. Mike saw lights behind him. He pulled over on the edge of the road. The officer approached the vehicle. Mike began to explain the situation. The officer crept back to his car with Mike's license and registration. Just as he was about to write him a ticket, he heard the dispatchers over the radio. He quickly walked back to Mike's jeep, gave him back his belongings and told him to keep up.

The officer pulled off and Mike pulled out behind him. The officer escorted him to the state line. Another trooper waited for him at the line to lead him across his state. Mike made phone calls to their families letting them know what had or could have potentially happened to her. As fast as he was going he was still an hour out. Back at the house Blue was indeed fighting. Big reached down and punched her in the stomach. She kicked him in the face knocking him over, kicking him again and again trying to put distance between them. She scrambled down the hall with him staggering behind her. She quickly made it to the closet. Fixated on choking her, he didn't see the gun in her hand. She pointed the barrel of the gun in his chest. They locked eyes. She saw the enjoyment in his face as he tried to cut off her airflow. She pulled the trigger.

The gun shot rang out through the house. He dropped her and he fell on top of her. She managed to push him off her. She drug herself across him and tried to leave out of the bedroom. He grabbed her leg and she kicked him with the other foot. He let her go. She crawled down the hall and tried to pull herself up. The police ran in the door. Before she passed out she recognized the officer as the one who escorted her home a few weeks ago. Big and Blue were both transported to the hospital. On the way, Blue began to have contractions. Baby Kristopher was trying to come. He still had a week and a half to go. The EMS workers had called ahead and let them know of her injuries. When she arrived Baby Kristopher was very distressed. The doctors could not find a heartbeat and ordered a C-section immediately.

The earth stood still as she replayed the encounter over in her head. She remembered the beautiful room and wondered if her baby would live to see it. Celeste and Delmar got the kids and set out to get to Blue. Ms. Bella made haste to her daughter and grandchild. Mr. and Mrs. Long broke laws as well getting to the hospital. Mike had given the dispatcher a description of the cars for the highway patrolmen to look for so they could be escorted in as well. Ms. Deb and Mr. Jim pulled up at the hospital the same time Mike did. They all rushed inside the hospital to be with Blue. This situation continued to spiral into a brutal hellish nightmare. Big was being prepped for surgery. They hurried Terrance him to the operating room.

The doctors were tasked with trying to stop the bleeding of the bullet that tore a large hole in his lung. Reporters were everywhere. Both Big and baby Kristopher were fighting for their lives. Baby Kristopher laid still and lifeless. They worked on him for some time trying to get him stable. They succeeded but it was touch and go for him for a moment. Kristopher began to show signs of movement and some life. As family arrived, they rushed in the hospital to find Mike and get answers on Blue and the baby. Blue had suffered some internal injuries from being kicked and hit during the fight. The doctor assured over time she would be fine. The doctor told them about the miracle of the baby and how he pulled through. Moments later the nurse brought him passed the waiting room on his way to the neonatal to be observed for the next couple of days.

As the nurse rolled the baby down the hall, Mike followed. The men followed him. The women waited for permission to join Blue's bedside. As the men walked behind the nurse and baby, they noticed Big being rolled from the opposite side of the hallway on his way to recovery. Mike saw him and charged towards him. The men grabbed Mike before he could approach Big. Breathing shallow with oxygen attached to his nose, he caught a glimpse of the baby. He and Mike locked eyes right before he had a seizure. He began to bleed losing blood and consciousness. They rushed him back to surgery. They opened his incision and tried to stop the bleeding. Before they could he'd bled out and flatlined. As death slipped way with his soul, the tag of baby Kristopher fell from his hand to the floor. It was over. Mike and Blue could finally live peacefully without the torture of Terrance Belton. Mike could freely raise Kristopher as he intended as his natural born son.

Acknowledgements

I would like to first off thank my God for allowing my gift to make room for me. My journey here has not been easy, there have been much sweat and many tears, but praise God I am making it through! I would like to thank my family for your love, support, and continued belief in me. Thank you to my supportive friends who are continued encouragement. Thank you to my fans, you guys are amazing!

Other Published Works

Blue Volume One

Check out my blog and

website at WWW.KSHARVIN.COM

About the Author

Keffney (Kat) S. Harvin was born in Greensboro North Carolina but raised in the humble town of Rockingham, North Carolina. She completed her first book (Blue Volume One) as an adult novelist, while continuing to be the devoted wife of a Highway Patrol Officer, the mother of three beautiful daughters, and "Nona" to one very precocious granddaughter. From teacher to writer Kat is continuing to shift her focus to her first love but holds a Child Development degree from North Carolina Agricultural and Technical State University and a Master of Art in Education Administration from the University of Grand Canyon. When not working on writing, blogging or music, Kat continues to enjoy singing, laughing with friends, and outreach. Blue Volume 2 is Keffney's continuation romantic novel, and the interaction between two men and woman are examined through the lenses of a young, assertive woman now that she has successfully found love. Sit back, grab another glass of wine, and enjoy the journey.